LEMMINGTOWN

LEMMINGTOWN

R.W. Mitchell

Copyright © 2022 by R.W. Mitchell.

Library of Congress Control Number: 2022903715
ISBN: Hardcover 978-1-6698-1155-8
Softcover 978-1-6698-1154-1
eBook 978-1-6698-1153-4

All rights reserved. No part of this book may be reproduced or transmitted in any form or by any means, electronic or mechanical, including photocopying, recording, or by any information storage and retrieval system, without permission in writing from the copyright owner.

This is a work of fiction. Names, characters, places and incidents either are the product of the author's imagination or are used fictitiously, and any resemblance to any actual persons, living or dead, events, or locales is entirely coincidental.

Any people depicted in stock imagery provided by Getty Images are models, and such images are being used for illustrative purposes only.
Certain stock imagery © Getty Images.

Print information available on the last page.

Cover Artwork by nskvsky.

Rev. date: 03/14/2022

To order additional copies of this book, contact:
Xlibris
844-714-8691
www.Xlibris.com
Orders@Xlibris.com
831944

Contents

Chapter 1	(Prologue)	1
Chapter 2	(Bigly's Bad Dream)	5
Chapter 3	(Bigly's Triumphant Return)	13
Chapter 4	(The Rise of Bigly)	20
Chapter 5	(Bigly's Scheme)	25
Chapter 6	(Tez's Search)	37
Chapter 7	(The Conception of Lemming City)	45
Chapter 8	(The Education of Tez)	55
Chapter 9	(Lemming City Nears Completion)	58
Chapter 10	(Return of the Legacies)	61
Chapter 11	(Two Worlds Collide)	69
Chapter 12	(The Grand Reveal)	77
Chapter 13	(The Fall of Lemming City)	94
Chapter 14	(Return to the Cliffs)	103

One

(Prologue)

Lemmingtown was a place like no other. It had been built countless generations before by a handful of founders, who were referred to simply as the *Ancients*. Little was known about them, other than the town they had created and the way of life they had passed down. Lemmingtown was the culmination of their wisdom, perseverance, and labor.

They had sought refuge from the harsh northern environment and the perils of predators like foxes, weasels, and snowy owls.

Owls could swoop down on any unsuspecting lemming who left itself exposed to the sky, and they struck like silent angels of death. Foxes were even more deadly. They could sniff out a lemming from hundreds of feet away. Unfortunately for lemmings, their tender flesh was considered a true delicacy—far more succulent than some scrawny mouse. Weasels posed no less a threat. They were adept at sneaking about and cramming their slender bodies into lemming tunnels, where they knew their next meal would be there for the taking.

Lemmings live in colonies which generally thrive for a handful of generations. But lemmings, by nature, spend much of their days feeding and mating. And as such prodigious breeders, populations inevitably grow out of control, and they eventually run out of food. When their habitat can no longer support them, most of the community has no choice other than to migrate in search of food. Their lifestyle leaves them victims of vicious cycles of boom and bust.

Lemmings are natural-born followers, and when they are compelled to relocate, they usually migrate in large groups. Contrary to popular belief, this is not some form of mass suicide. They simply follow one another in a blind search for a new home. Most of them are either eaten or die on arduous journeys. Many long lines of lemmings have been known to follow one another, attempting to swim across impossibly wide rivers or accidentally plunging over the tops of high cliffs.

A few, however, occasionally manage to survive.

Whether it was by destiny or serendipity or just dumb luck, this was how Lemmingtown had come to be. It was built near a high clifftop where refugee lemmings were unknowingly streaming over the edge and plunging to their deaths.

But there were a few who thought differently—they were not mere followers—and they had stopped short of the precipice.

They decided to build a new and better life.

Nothing about what would become life in Lemmingtown had happened by chance or good fortune because it was the result of careful consideration and serious debate. They shared a vision and wanted something more permanent. It was to be something that would last beyond the next inevitable bust. The Ancients set out to live a more disciplined life—it was to be one of modesty and self-control. It was to be a community of moderation in everything they did, particularly when it came to mating, because each summer a typical female lemming can give birth to as many as three litters of three or four young.

And thus, Lemmingtown was born.

They built a vast system of tunnels and chambers which were located deep underground. It was deep enough so that foxes could never hear them nor sniff them out. The tunnels they constructed incorporated sharp turns with traps that would bring a swift end to any invading weasel.

Lemmingtown was created as a sanctuary, but it grew into much more than that— it became a way of life. There was no formal government, nor were there any hard and fast rules. Each contributed in their own way, and everyone had a role to play. There were tunnellers, gatherers, and sentries, who were always standing guard to warn of any approaching predator.

The Ancients had also bestowed a sense of decency on the community. Of course, you took care of yourself but never at the expense of another. There were always bound to be minor quarrels, but the community was thriving, and almost everyone in Lemmingtown was happy to share with one another and always more than willing to lend a helping hand.

Tez, for instance, was an exemplary young female. She was excellent in character and a model citizen. She was a hardworking food gatherer who always strove to serve others. She embodied the vision of the Ancients.

But as in any society, Lemmingtown was also saddled with its share of bad actors, and Bigly was easily the worst offender. He was the polar opposite of Tez and embodied all that the Ancients would have abhorred.

Bigly considered himself above the community and thought everyone else to be weak and nothing more than easy marks to exploit. He was big and fat and lazy, with limited intelligence. He was a natural-born shirker who excelled at dodging his responsibilities. But he was also adept at talking his way out of any kind of trouble. He wasn't particularly skilled at anything other than his natural ability to manipulate others and had managed to cheat his way through life but always in a remarkably charming manner.

And when you placed a character like that in Lemmingtown, where everyone else was so willing to help one another, and combined it with lemmings' natural tendency to follow, it added up to a recipe for trouble.

Two

(Bigly's Bad Dream)

Bigly woke up in a panic late one night. He'd had a vivid dream that the entire town had finally caught on to him, and he realized they probably wouldn't let him get away with all his shirking much longer. He knew he had to act immediately to prevent the inevitable and came up with a simple plan—although it was really more of a scheme.

He decided to try to ingratiate himself with the colony by creating the illusion that he was actually a hard worker. He figured if he worked hard for a short time, he might be able to ride on everyone's new perception of him and then coast again for as long as he could, falling back on his same lame excuses. And the more he thought of it, the more he liked his plan.

Bigly was supposed to be a gatherer, but he rarely gathered.

So on that morning, instead of trying to pawn off his duties with some made-up excuse of injury or illness, he hurried outside with the others to gather food just after sunrise. While many of them were pleasantly surprised by his apparent newfound enthusiasm, more than a few were suspicious.

Bigly worked feverishly gathering shoots of moss and other plants as well as small pieces of bark and twigs for bedding, though he did spend a fair amount of his time guzzling the best of the food as he collected it.

Gatherers were always careful to never stray far from the tunnel entrance, where a handful of sentries, often older and less agile lemmings, kept a watchful eye for predators. The gatherers scurried out and back from the entrance where others were standing by to ferry the harvest into caverns deep inside the tunnel.

On one of the trips out from the entrance, Bigly ran into Spencer. He was agreeable enough but with a milquetoast personality. The pair hit it off right away because Bigly wasn't keen on lemmings with strong characters or sharp minds. On the way back out, Spencer introduced him to Derk, who was much livelier but not particularly clever either.

Everything had gone smoothly that morning, and with the exception of a few false alarms, all the gatherers eventually headed back underground with their last collection of the day.

Bigly headed out again the following morning with even more gusto than the day before. It didn't take long before he tried to coax Spencer and Derk to venture out a further.

"Everything out here is so picked over," Bigly said. "Why don't we try going out a little further?"

"But what about the foxes?" Spencer asked.

"What about them? Nobody's seen one in weeks."

"How would you know?" Derk asked. "We hardy ever see you out here."

"Oh, everybody knows that. That's all they've been talking about," Bigly said, making everything up as he went along.

"I'm still not sure it's a good idea," Spencer said.

"But just think how pleased everyone would be with what we might bring back," Bigly said. "Don't worry. We'll be careful, and I bet we bring back more than all the rest of them combined."

Bigly had played them well because it didn't take much more prodding for Derk and Spencer to be persuaded, and they all scurried out further than was prudent.

Bigly had been right in his hunch, and they managed to gather an enormous amount of delicious food—so much, in fact, that they could scarcely drag all of it back.

When they finally arrived at the tunnel entrance, the other gatherers were astonished at their haul. The three of them basked in all the attention and admiration of the others.

Bigly felt a boost to his ego like never before, and it left him wanting more.

Bigly had been proven right, and his plan looked like it might already be beginning to work. He was pretty sure it wouldn't take long before he could get back to shirking his responsibilities again.

Later that night, Bigly reveled in his newfound approval. He chatted with all the other gatherers, including Dweezil, who wouldn't have even given him the time of day just the day before.

Dweezil was scrawny, pale, and aptly named—he actually looked like he might have been part weasel, and there was something conniving about him. The two of them spoke excitedly, and it wasn't long before Spencer and Derk joined the conversation.

"You see," Bigly said, "I'm sure there's so much more to be taken out there. We just have to have the courage to go out and get it."

"Are you sure?" Spencer asked. "What do you think, Derk?"

"Well, part of me says maybe we were just lucky not to have been eaten."

"It's not luck," Dweezil said. "And Bigly's right. Just look at the foxes. They take anything they want, whenever they want it."

"But they're foxes," Spencer said, "and we're just lemmings."

Bigly smiled and said, "I'm tired of being weak, and I'm tired of being afraid of being preyed upon. We need to start acting more like foxes and less like lemmings. And just imagine how much respect we'll get from pulling it off again. And you know, with respect comes privilege."

None of them could help but liking the sound of *gaining privilege*, and the more they thought of it, the more they liked the idea of garnering undeserved attention.

Bigly had cleverly begun to surround himself with like-minded lemmings.

"We'll just need to be more clever than a fox," Derk said.

"Yes, we need to outsmart our enemy," Bigly said.

"Exactly," Dweezil said, "We need to . . . you know . . . outfox them."

"That's it! Outfox the foxes!" Bigly said. "Oh, I do like that. Outfox the foxes!"

He broke into a big grin and said, "Tomorrow we are going to outfox the foxes!"

"Outfox the foxes," they all echoed back.

Dweezil joined Bigly and his gang early the next morning, and they ventured out even further than before—well beyond where any reasonable lemming would even consider going.

Bigly led the way but could sense that the others were getting worried, so he turned back and yelled, "Outfox the foxes!"

"Outfox the foxes," they all chanted back, each trying to appear braver than they actually were so as to not to appear weak to Bigly nor embarrass themselves in front of one another.

Little did they know what lay ahead.

About a hundred feet downwind, Mr. Sid, an alpha male, and four vixen were busy pouncing on any unfortunate mouse who happened by and were having a rather good morning.

Mr. Sid was more cunning than most other foxes and could have a particularly nasty side to him if provoked. Even the grey wolves respected him and rarely ever tried to attack. The vixen knew this and loved him for it because he made them feel safe.

Mr. Sid suddenly stopped hunting and raised his snout.

He knew the unmistakable scent of lemming and breathed it in deeply. It had been a long time since he'd had a whiff of lemming. The vixen followed his lead. They all could vaguely hear something in the distance, and all their ears pricked up.

Mr. Sid tilted his head to one side and could scarcely believe what he was hearing.

"Did you hear that?" he asked. "Outfox the foxes? Oh, that is rich, isn't it, ladies?"

The vixen giggled and went to work in a flash. They spread out and began to encircle the unsuspecting lemmings.

Angel, a snowy owl, was circling high above and spotted the foxes moving into formation. Angel rarely had any trouble finding her next meal, but it never hurt to have a fellow predator tip its hand from below.

Mr. Sid saw her shadow streak across the ground and took note—no bird was going to steal his lunch.

The foxes crept in slowly, keeping low to the ground, and surprised the lemmings as if they had come out of nowhere. Their chanting stopped right after "out" and just before "fox." Mr. Sid yelped and the vixen stopped dead in their tracks. Mr. Sid looked up and saw that Angel was about to swoop down and said, "Not yet ladies." They knew exactly what he meant and moved in closer to protect the lemmings but drooling nevertheless.

Bigly's gang stood trembling. Bigly tried to look calm and fearless, even though he was scared senseless as well.

Mr. Sid moved in closer.

Bigly had seen Angel's shadow flash behind Mr. Sid another time.

"Wait!" he said. "Thank you for saving us from that owl, Mr. Fox! We owe you our lives."

"Don't worry," Mr. Sid said. "We were just about to get to that."

Dweezil, Derk, and Spencer began shaking even more violently.

One of the vixen, Vanessa, pressed her snout against Dweezil and took a deep breath of his sweet aroma.

"Now, Vanessa," Mr. Sid said calmly, "not yet, my darling."

She knew better than upsetting Mr. Sid. Maybe he wanted this one. Maybe he even wanted all of them. The other vixen knew better too.

"I believe we might have a bit of a problem here," Bigly said after clearing his throat.

"No. I believe *you* have a bit of a problem here," Mr. Sid replied coolly.

"But don't you see it?" Bigly asked. "There's only four of us, but there's five of you."

"And?"

"Someone's going to be left empty-handed."

"Too bad," Mr. Sid said.

"But what if I have an idea that would deliver you a hundred times our number? There are five of you, right? So let's say five a day for starters, every single day. And I can even have them come right to your doorstep."

"I might be hungry," Mr. Sid said, "but I'm still listening."

Bigly thought himself a sharp negotiator, but the only reason the four of them hadn't been devoured already was because Mr. Sid and his vixen were already satiated after such a successful morning. Besides, he could still eat all of them later if he changed his mind.

Bigly had suspected that Mr. Sid might like shortcuts as much as he did, and if he was right, he might be willing to spare Bigly and his gang for the prospect of an abundance of easy meals.

Bigly went on to explain how important he was in his town and about his vision to expand it and how there'd be an abundance of lemmings working for him in the field, and if there happened to be any *accidents*, well, that would be just a small price to pay for progress.

"When's all this going to happen?" Mr. Sid asked.

"Soon," Bigly said. "Very soon. You'll see. Deal?"

Mr. Sid paused long enough for a large drop of sweat to dribble down Bigly's forehead and then said, "Deal."

Bigly was shocked and relieved and began to swell with pride. He truly had outfoxed the foxes.

That was until Mr. Sid added, "For now."

Bigly gulped.

Mr. Sid nodded to the vixen, and they backed away. Vanessa let out a disappointed whimper.

Bigly's gang had been in such shock they hadn't heard any of what had just transpired. All they could do was to scurry away behind their leader.

To them, Bigly was a genius who had somehow managed to save their skins, and they would now follow him anywhere.

Bigly smiled a big stupid smile.

The vixen looked disappointed and confused as they watched their quarry disappear into the woods.

They all turned toward Mr. Sid.

"Follow them," he said.

Three

(Bigly's Triumphant Return)

Bigly led the way back to town but stopped them to gather as much food as they could carry because he knew *he'd* look bad if they returned with anything less than the day before.

How clever I am, he thought. *I'm going to be a legend, and from now on, these idiots are going to follow me anywhere.* He chuckled to himself and flashed an even broader and stupider smile.

Just as they were about to reach the entrance to the town, Bigly fell back a little while the others continued on. He paused for a moment and turned back. He spotted Vanessa and the others trailing them but not attacking. The foxes now had a pretty good idea where Lemmingtown lay, and Bigly knew he now *had* to deliver on his deal with Mr. Sid.

They entered the tunnel, and Saggy was standing guard just a few feet inside. He was a wrinkly old lemming with great drooping jowls and flabby neck.

"What took you so long?" he asked.

"Bit of a snag back there," Bigly replied casually.

"Don't you think you're being reckless? You're acting completely irresponsibly, and I think it's dangerous. You've got half the other gatherers thinking about heading out further."

Dweezil, who was finally recovering from the shock of their encounter with the foxes, couldn't resist and blurted out, "You won't believe what just happened!"

"What do you mean?" Saggy asked.

"We were surrounded by five vicious foxes and got away!"

"You're right. I don't believe it. You were probably all off shirking somewhere."

"No, it's true," Spencer said. "Just look at everything we brought back."

"So you really expect me to believe that the four of *you* managed to escape from five vicious foxes? Really?" Saggy said. "How?"

"I can't really remember because it all happened so fast," Spencer said. "It's all a bit of a blur to me now."

"So you're telling me you somehow managed to get away from five vicious foxes and can't even remember how?"

"We outfoxed the foxes," Derk said coolly.

"That's right," Spencer added. "We outfoxed the foxes!"

"No!" Dweezil said. "Bigly outfoxed the foxes! The two of you were too busy shaking like babies!"

"Listen to him!" Derk said. "I thought you were going to pass out."

"Bigly?" Saggy asked sternly.

"Well, it's a bit of a long story," Bigly said.

He knew Saggy was skeptical and was already asking far too many questions, but he had a hunch that his fabrication would play out far better in front of a larger audience.

"Why don't we go to one of the rooms so I can share our story with everyone?" he suggested.

They scurried down the entrance tunnel and zigzagged their way further inside, finally making their way for one of the large rooms further ahead.

A group of morning gatherers had been lingering around inside, curious if Bigly and the others would ever return. They had been engrossed in an odd combination of idle chatter, wild speculation, and outlandish theories about what might have become of them.

Seamus, who had always been inclined to the bizarre, had initially raised the possibility of poachers. Legend had it that there were giant creatures who walked upright on their hind legs and prized the hides of lemmings, and if one of these beasts ever spotted you, you'd be scooped up and never be heard from again. Most of the group had initially dismissed the idea, but more than a few had started to think that maybe they shouldn't dismiss it after all. Carson, who always adopted strong and unfounded opinions, couldn't agree more.

Anders, a pure-white-haired lemming, was much more attached to reality. He thought they had most likely strayed too far from the entrance and simply fallen victim to any of the usual predators, such as a fox or an owl, and wondered out loud what could have possessed them to venture so far out in the first place. Jake, a like-minded lemming, agreed.

Lanky, a stretched-out female, who was always more concerned with her appearance than anything else, had overheard some of Bigly's views the night before and had bought into his idea that there was much more to be taken further afield. She believed that the four of them had merely been delayed and would soon return with an abundance of riches.

Each had their own opinion, but there was definitely a growing concern that the group might never return.

The gatherers had become so engrossed in all their speculation that they didn't notice when Bigly and his gang arrived at the door. Saggy cleared his throat, but nobody noticed, so he hollered out, "Hey, everybody! They're back."

"It's Bigly!" Lanky screamed, and everyone turned toward the entrance.

Lanky was young and attractive and had that certain quality that attracted every male in town. Bigly noticed her immediately and beamed his best smile her way—this time not so big and not so stupid-looking. He was charming, and she was enthralled.

Bigly knew he was in business now, and it wouldn't take long to have this entire crowd in the palm of his hand.

They raced toward the entrance which was elevated above the rest of the room. The cavern resonated with wild chatter of "Bigly's back!" and "They really made it!"

They peppered Bigly with questions about what had happened. Spencer, Derk, and Dweezil stood silently by the door, with Saggy watching on from behind.

The crowd fell silent, and Bigly stepped forward.

"Friends," he said, "it was really quite a morning."

The gatherers fell silent, and Bigly paused. "Today we outfoxed the foxes."

"No!" Dweezil yelled. "Bigly outfoxed the foxes! And we owe him our lives!"

The group erupted into agitated chatter with surprised calls like "Bigly outfoxed foxes?"

Lanky shrieked, "Bigly outfoxed the foxes!"

"What happened?" Seamus and Carson shouted out above the ruckus.

Bigly leaned forward and continued. "Well, friends, as I was saying, it really was quite a morning."

The crowd, still shocked at his return after all their speculation, offered up a little polite laughter.

"Yes, quite a morning."

The crowd was enthralled and anxious to hear more, and Bigly knew it.

"I led my brave companions well past the safety of where most other lemmings would ever dare. I believe in pushing everything as far as possible. I believe in taking everything to the limit, even if it means risking everything. Because where there is risk, there is also reward!"

"Tell us more!" Seamus shouted.

"Don't stop now!" Carson added.

Bigly paused a moment to allow more tension to build then continued.

"We had ventured deep into the frontier. Were we worried? Were we afraid? Of course, we were. It would be crazy not to be. But our goal, no, indeed our *mission*, was so important to us that we had to press on. We were careful to remain silent as we pushed deeper and deeper into the frontier. And let me tell you this: There is an abundance of riches out there. And it's all ours, just waiting for the taking."

"Too dangerous for me," somebody grumbled from the back of the room.

"You must be fearless!" another shouted.

Bigly chuckled and added, "Dangerous? Yes, but we knew the prize."

Anders turned to Jake and said, "This guy's nuts."

Jake just shook his head and rolled his eyes as Bigly carried on.

"Suddenly, and completely out of nowhere, we were surrounded by vicious foxes!"

There was a collective gasp from the crowd.

"I couldn't even tell you how many there were, but we were vastly outnumbered. I knew we had to act, and we had to act fast. Our very lives depended on it!"

The crowd was hanging on his every word, and Bigly was becoming intoxicated with being the center of attention. He was brimming with pride and absolutely dying to flash a big stupid smile but knew better this time.

"For me," he said, "it was as if everything started to happen in slow motion. I spotted a rabbit hole to the right, not far from the smallest of the foxes, and it came to me in a flash. I knew the boys could make a break for it if I provided some kind of distraction. So I did the unexpected." He held another long pause before continuing. "I bared my teeth and charged straight at those foxes, screaming louder than I've ever screamed in my life! The foxes were so startled that they hesitated just long enough for the boys to take flight as I threw myself down the rabbit hole."

The crowd was eating it up, and Bigly knew it. He was beginning to realize the power of his own voice.

Dweezil yelled, "Bigly outfoxed the foxes!"

The crowd erupted into chants of "Outfoxed the foxes!"

Lanky was giddy beyond belief. She was just as intoxicated with Bigly as he was with being the center of attention. And she wasn't the only one. Almost everyone else in the room was equally enthralled.

Jake turned back to Anders and said, "He's not nuts. He's just making all this up."

"Maybe he's up to something," Anders said.

"I don't know," Jake said, "I doubt he's clever enough."

Bigly's deal with Mr. Sid was still in the back of his mind, and he figured he was on such a roll, there'd never be a better time to unveil his zany plan to expand the town.

He carried on, making up all of it as he went along.

"Even though there are risks, the rewards will be enormous!"

Even the most cautious and skeptical of gatherers had now stopped thinking for themselves, as if having been infected by something beyond their control, and they began cheering.

"We can make this happen. Starting right now. There's a whole new frontier out there, and it's all ours for the taking!"

"What about the foxes?" Anders shouted.

Jake and others echoed the objection.

"Not a problem at all," Bigly said calmly. "Just leave them to me. I outfoxed them this morning, and I can outfox them again."

The room broke back into wild cheers.

Bigly instinctively knew his pitch would work best by leaving them wanting more, so he silenced everyone and concluded by saying, "It was a long morning, so why don't we all meet back here again later tonight? I want to share more of my ideas with you. And bring your friends! I think you're all going to love what I have to say."

Four

(The Rise of Bigly)

Word of Bigly's feat had spread like wildfire though the town, and later that night, the same room was absolutely overflowing with lemmings. Bigly came through the entrance, flanked by his gang, which now included Lanky and Saggy. The room fell silent, and all the lemmings stepped aside as he made his way to the front.

Bigly turned back to the crowd, and they erupted into wild cheers. The cheering, even from what was only a modest group, was almost deafening in the cramped space. What started out with chants of "Outfoxed the foxes! Outfoxed the foxes!" soon turned into "Bigly! Bigly! Bigly!" over and over.

Bigly knew he had played his cards well, and now it was showtime!

He retold the story of how he had outfoxed the foxes with flair and drama and even more embellishment on top of what had already been a complete fabrication, aside from his unintentional and somewhat ironic reference to the rabbit hole he had actually plunged himself into. He was truly a master of innately knowing how to spin a story to make himself look far better than actuality.

He hinted at his plans to grow Lemmingtown and how there was an abundance of riches to be had, just as he had done earlier. But again, it was without any real specifics other than he would reveal it all the following night in the Great Hall. He made a grand exit from the room to the chants of "Bigly, Bigly, Bigly!"

Saggy, who had been standing against the wall to one side of the room, had lain awake all night, thinking about what he had witnessed. He was sure he'd never seen anything quite like it before. He knew, deep down, what Bigly was really all about and seriously doubted anything he had heard was even close to reality. But he also saw something else. He saw the power that Bigly could wield. And just like Lanky, he wanted to be a part of whatever it was that was going on. He wanted Bigly's attention—any attention at all.

Saggy had barely managed to squeeze in a couple of hours of sleep by morning, but he woke up feeling refreshed. He was invigorated. He was, in fact, a whole new lemming. He didn't even bother to eat anything from his stash of food. He just scurried off to find Dweezil and the others.

He ran into Seamus and Carson who were talking excitedly. Bigly's tales seemed to have had the same profound effect on them. They too felt truly alive for the first time in a very long time. It was like they all had been shaken out of some kind of sleepy malaise. They had shared the Bigly experience, and they all wanted more.

"Hey, Saggy," Seamus called. "You're in a big hurry for an old guy."

"What are you?" Carson asked. "Hungry or something?"

"No!" he said. "I'm too excited to eat. I'm off to find Dweezil. Have you seen him?"

"He's around here somewhere," Carson said. "We were just talking to him a minute ago."

"Bigly sure put on some show last night, didn't he?" Seamus said.

"I hardly slept a wink," Saggy said.

"Neither did we," Carson said.

"He's like a breath of fresh air," Seamus said.

"And you know," Saggy said, "I've been feeling somehow bored and somehow stuck in a rut until now. But for the first time in a very long time, I'm actually excited about the future."

"Us too," Seamus said.

"That's why we've got to spread the word," Saggy said. "I feel something really big is going to happen in Lemmingtown, and I want to be part of it. I want to be part of history."

"We know," Seamus said.

"That's all we've been talking about!" Carson said.

"And that's exactly why I'm off to find Dweezil," Saggy said.

He scurried down the tunnel and peered inside the first room on his left, but it was empty. A little further on, in a room to the right, he spotted Dweezil and the others, including Lanky, who had brought along a group of her friends. They were all visibly excited about the night before and couldn't wait to see Bigly's next performance.

This is amazing, Saggy thought, *and it's going to be bigger than anything I could have ever imagined.*

Dweezil had been recounting Bigly's tale from the night before, and he'd taken the liberty of embellishing it even further. It couldn't have been easier because he couldn't remember anything about what had happened that day anyway—besides the being surrounded by foxes part—and his revised version was playing well to the group.

Just as he was about to finish his version of the story, he noticed Saggy standing at the entrance and quickly added, "And if wasn't for Saggy, we might never have made it back into the tunnel . . . Oh look! Here he is now."

Lanky and her friends turned toward the entrance and rushed toward him. Saggy was caught completely off guard—had he become some kind of overnight celebrity too? A rush of endorphins flooded his brain. He had never experienced any kind of attention even remotely like this before, and it was thrilling.

But before they even had the chance to speak to Saggy, Dweezil forced himself between all of them to prevent Saggy from saying anything that might derail his story. He turned back to the group and said, "Friends, what we need now is for all of you to get out and spread the word! Bigly is planning a gathering in the Great Hall tonight, and we need as many lemmings as we can get to join us. So get out and tell everyone you know. Bigly is counting on you! And always remember, Bigly outfoxed the foxes!"

How clever, Dweezil thought. He knew that Saggy had been skeptical of Bigly's story from the beginning, but he sensed that a little attention from some strangers just might bring him around. *I'll need to tell Bigly about this*, he thought, with hopes of ingratiating himself further.

Everyone in the group scattered off in their separate ways, each excited by the story they had just heard. They too wanted something new and exciting in their lives. And here it was, all served up and handed to them: Bigly had outfoxed the foxes!

Saggy turned to Dweezil and asked, "What was that about?"

"I was explaining how you had to rush us into the tunnels and back into the safety of Lemmingtown."

"What are you talking about?" Saggy asked, confused by what had just happened but still savoring the rush he had felt.

"Look," Dweezil said, "we might have looked calm on the outside, but we were still badly shaken by what we'd been through. Who knows? We might have got confused at the entrance and fallen into a trap. You saved us!"

"Well," Saggy said modestly, "if you put it that way, well, then yes. I suppose I really did help you, didn't I?"

"Yes, you did. You most certainly did," Dweezil said.

Saggy had taken the bait.

"You know," Saggy said, "I was very skeptical about Bigly's story at first—"

Dweezil interrupted before he could finish his sentence, "How could it not be true if I wasn't standing right in front of you?"

"You're right!" Saggy said. "Bigly really did outfox the foxes, didn't he? Yes, I see it now. Bigly outfoxed the foxes!"

Mission accomplished. Dweezil only wished that Bigly had been there to see it for himself, the second time in as many minutes.

Saggy continued, "And I've seen the effect he has on everyone and how they love him. He's exactly what we all need right now. He's like a breath of fresh air."

Five

(Bigly's Scheme)

Bigly had stayed up all night planning his next steps—although scheming would have been a better way to describe it. He was going to start enlisting volunteers to begin exploring the frontier and take a proper survey of the surrounding lands. He knew it might be difficult to find more than a handful to venture outside the safety of the town, even though he was riding a wave of popularity.

He had already summoned Dweezil and the rest of his gang to meet early the next morning, and when they arrived, he began outlining his plans.

"I think we need to . . .," he said, "you know, make all this sound somehow better, somehow more compelling."

They all fell silent for a moment, reflecting on what Bigly had just said.

An inspiration suddenly struck Dweezil like a bolt of lightning, and he blurted out, "Let's tell them they're going to be *pioneers* . . . no, they're going to be *heroes*!"

"Yes," Bigly said, "they're going to be heroes!"

Bigly's mind began to race, and he screamed out, "No, wait! We're going to call them the *New Ancients*!"

"That's brilliant!" Spencer said.

"No wonder you outfoxed the foxes!" Derk added.

"Well, it's all set then. You spread the word about the gathering, while I work out a few other details and prepare my speech," Bigly said.

They were all completely oblivious to the irony in the term *New Ancients*, which bordered on oxymoronic. Even trying to bury its absurdity in a term like *Neo-Ancients*, which might have sounded more sophisticated, would still amount to nothing more than thin veneer on top of Bigly's nefarious intent.

Bigly was cunning enough to realize it would be a recipe for disaster if the first wave of suckers who ventured out of town were immediately devoured by foxes. On the other hand, if he didn't stick to his deal with Mr. Sid, he too would eventually meet the same fate, and he simply wasn't going to allow that to happen.

It was still morning when he decided to venture back to the place where he had made his deal with Mr. Sid to ask him for more time.

When he arrived, it didn't take long before he was surrounded by foxes once again. Luckily for Bigly, one of them was Vanessa, and she recognized him immediately. She had been out training young foxes and helping them hone their hunting skills.

Just as one of them was about to pounce on Bigly, Vanessa snarled—he always seemed to somehow escape everything. It was as if he had some kind of Teflon coating.

"Leave it alone. This one's mine," she said threateningly.

She turned back to Bigly and asked, "You again?"

Bigly shuddered.

"What about your deal with Mr. Sid? What is this? Some kind of joke? Nobody wants to eat you, you little fat twerp. Where's our five a day like you promised?"

"Wait," Bigly said, "I need to see Mr. Sid right away."

Vanessa, forever loyal and obedient to Mr. Sid, complied. But it was not without first licking the saliva dripping from her lips.

She escorted Bigly back to the den with the young foxes following behind, careful to protect Bigly from other predators, who, no doubt, had either caught scent of him or had already spotted him. Angel, the snowy owl, probably posed the greatest threat, and Vanessa had already seen her shadow flash by several times. She grabbed Bigly gently in her mouth and carried him the rest of the way back to the den. It caught Bigly completely by surprise, and he was terrified for the rest of the trip.

As they neared the den, Bigly began to feel rather good—very good, in fact. Perhaps not quite like the night before, but a sense of power was gradually welling up inside him. *It's all about attitude*, he thought. He was about to meet the ruler of the foxes for the second time, and he now knew exactly what he wanted most. He wanted to rule the lemmings—he wanted to rule Lemmingtown. He had made up his mind, and nobody was going to stop him now. Nobody.

Mr. Sid was lounging inside the den and had surrounded himself with a half dozen young vixen when Vanessa brought Bigly inside. Mr. Sid didn't even bother to move as she dumped Bigly on the floor in front of him.

"Oh good," Mr. Sid said, "here's my breakfast."

"No," Vanessa said, "this is that Bigly character you let get away the other day."

"Oh him," Mr. Sid said.

Bigly's heart sank a little because he longed to be liked by Mr. Sid—the same way Bigly's followers wanted to be noticed by him. Bigly sank low to the ground, as if bowing, and said humbly, "You spared my life, Mr. Fox, sir, and as I promised, I am working very hard to repay the profound debt I owe you. I am now and will forever be in your service."

He didn't really like groveling because it made him feel weak, but he sensed he needed to win over Mr. Sid if he was ever to rule Lemmingtown.

Mr. Sid had already started salivating, and while his canine instincts were to just pounce on the fat little lemming right there and then, he knew better. Besides, if he didn't like what Bigly had to say, he could always eat him later, just like before.

"Go ahead. I'm listening," he said.

Bigly went on at great length, yet again, meandering around his plans for expanding Lemmingtown and about all the great success he'd had in convincing everyone to join him in such a short time. He pressed hard to convince Mr. Sid how his plans would eventually deliver a huge victory for him and all his foxes in the months ahead.

"Think of it," Bigly said, "as I grow my town, I will send more and more explorers out here, into what we call the *frontier*, and you will be blessed with an abundance of meals walking right to your front door."

"Why would they do that?" Mr. Sid asked.

"Do what?" Bigly asked back, apparently completely oblivious to the fact that he was in the middle of selling out his town for the second time. The only thing he was thinking about was gaining absolute power, the same kind of absolute power Mr. Sid obviously held.

"To leave your puny little town and be eaten by us," Mr. Sid replied.

Bigly realized that Mr. Sid didn't understand where his plan was leading, and while he was a little surprised, he was more delighted than anything else. He really and truly did know how to outfox the foxes, and he spotted an opening.

"Of course," he said, "but the most important thing is to build up a sense of security first. That way, more and more explorers will venture out into the frontier. And if a few go missing . . . well, so be it. We will thank them and praise them as fallen heroes. So all I'm asking for is a little time."

"Hmm," Mr. Sid said, still lounging with his harem. "That might work. Maybe I underestimated you. You seem to think like a fox."

Bigly felt a gush of pride swell inside himself.

Mr. Sid paused and said, "No big deal anyway."

"Why not?" Bigly asked.

"Because I know where you live."

He paused to lick the stream of drool spilling over his lips.

Vanessa had been sitting silently at the entrance to the den but had paid close attention to everything in the exchange. Her admiration for Mr. Sid was swelling more than ever, and she was absorbing everything that had just transpired. She was cut from the same cloth as Mr. Sid and knew that if she were patient enough, her turn to lead might arrive one day.

A little later, Vanessa and a few other of Mr. Sid's vixen escorted Bigly back to Lemmingtown, always protecting him from all the other predators lurking in the forest and in the sky.

Yes, Bigly thought to himself. *I really have outfoxed the foxes. I have outfoxed everyone!*

When he arrived home, Bigly started to prepare for his speech but quickly grew tired of the work. *What do I need to prepare for?* he thought. *I am Bigly, and I'll just make it up as I go. It always comes out better that way anyway.*

Bigly entered the Great Hall that evening, late as always to add a flair of drama.

The hall was filled to capacity and buzzing with gossip which charged it up with a strange sort of energy—even more electric than the night before.

The room had been scraped out by the Ancients and had been intended for more solemn occasions, but Bigly had no interest in decorum. He had become an overnight celebrity and knew he could get away with anything he liked.

He climbed onto the stage and stepped forward. The crowd fell silent. He spotted Saggy near the front and pointed at him and smiled, which Saggy felt thrilling. Everyone was enthralled and anxious to hear everything he had to share with them. Bigly felt the beginnings of the same kind of rush he'd experienced the night before—only this time it was ten times more powerful, and he was loving every second of it.

The time had come to sell the town on the preposterous idea that he had cooked up in front of Mr. Sid, but he was cunning enough to know that he first had to whip them into a frenzy before he had any chance of garnering any recruits to venture out into the frontier. He had already prepared a witty response to anyone who might think it too dangerous: "What are you? Are you a lemming? Or are you a mouse?"

And so he launched into another completely predictable rant. "Friends," he started but had to stop for a moment because the crowd had erupted again. Endorphins were flooding his brain, building lockstep with the growing adoration of *his* lemmings.

The din gradually died down, and he continued, "My friends, I think it's fair to say that things in Lemmingtown are finally going much, much better now."

The crowd cheered again at this utter insanity—nothing had changed at all—but at this point, they would cheer at anything Bigly said because they had all simply fallen under his spell.

He eventually hit his stride and talked at length about the Ancients and all the hardships they had to endure and how this great opportunity had been handed to him as if by destiny.

"Our town is now the greatest in the land, and while we might owe something to the Ancients . . .," pausing for a dramatically long time, "we need to reach even further. Together, we will make Lemmingtown bigger. We will make it better! We will make it stronger!"

The crowd thundered its approval, and then Bigly's voice took on a serious tone.

"I have always looked to the future. I have studied the Ancient texts for my entire life, and I know more about them than anyone. But I'm afraid that I have to tell you that I don't like what I see lying ahead."

While it was true that the Ancients had created texts countless generations before, all that remained were scarcely more than fragments, and even if read carefully, they could be interpreted in any number of ways. Furthermore, it wasn't entirely clear if the fragments were even the genuine work of the Ancients, rather than interpretations of what was thought they might have intended, written long after the fact.

But none of it really mattered because Bigly couldn't even read.

"The texts warn us that food shortages may be around the corner. This is a grave threat, and I'm not just making this up. The threat is real, and we can't afford to ignore it any longer! We need to explore! We need to expand! We need to seek out new territory! I have seen the new lands with my own eyes, and there is more than enough food to feed all of us forever. It's all next door, and it's all ours for the taking. We are going to build a bigger and better Lemmingtown, and we are going to start today!"

Bigly paused again and chuckled a little. Then he continued, "I don't know about you, but I'm tired of all this living in moderation. I want to eat and breed when *I* decide—like any normal lemming would want to do. It's what lemmings were born to do! It's only natural, and I know exactly how we can do it! We explore, and we expand. It's just that simple."

Bigly had finally managed to work the crowd into a frenzy.

"I see the future!" he yelled. "*I* am the future of Lemmingtown! And I promise you I will save Lemmingtown!"

The crowd again erupted into screams of "Bigly! Bigly! Bigly!"

Anyone would normally brush this off as the ravings of a lunatic, but for some inexplicable reason, the crowd was eating it up. It was as if the crowd couldn't care less about anything he had to say—they just wanted to be part of this movement, no matter how crazy it sounded. And Bigly knew it.

"And that is why, my friends, I solemnly swear that I will change this town. I am going to make it great! Greater than you could possibly imagine. Greater than your wildest dreams!"

Bigly's fur was now completely drenched in sweat, and he was beginning to run out of steam, but the crowd, which was growing wilder by the second, broke into chanting all over the Great Room. On one side, "Bigly, Bigly, Bigly!" was echoed with "Outfoxed the foxes!" on the other.

It gave him a boost of energy like never before. Bigly nodded along with the chanting, albeit a little off the beat.

He finally launched into the pitch that he had concocted earlier that morning, about how any lemming brave enough to volunteer would be a true hero and would go down in history as one of the New Ancients and be celebrated forever.

What Bigly liked best about all the mayhem was that the crazier it got, the less anyone paid any attention to anything that he was saying. In fact, much of the time he didn't even know what he was talking about himself. But what did it matter? The crowd loved it, and they loved him. All the chanting and adoration stoked his ego, and he was fully recharged in almost no time, so he decided to keep on going.

The crowd rushed to the stage to get a closer look at Bigly—to brush with his celebrity and feel the same rush that Bigly had felt from the moment he had taken the stage. They too desperately wanted to be part of history.

And if they followed Bigly, they most certainly would—for better or worse.

But not everyone in the hall was equally enthralled, and a handful of skeptics had been lingering at the back of the crowd. None of them could understand all the excitement that Bigly was capable of generating with his nonsensical rhetoric and theatrics.

Tez had been standing off to one side with her lifelong friends Kit and Finn, two other fine young lemmings. Just across them were Anders and Jake, who were shaking their heads in disbelief at the spectacle they were witnessing. They spotted Tez and her friends and waved them over. They were keen to see if anyone else shared their views but were completely open to be convinced otherwise.

"So what did you young lemmings make of that?" Jake asked, shouting above the din still echoing through the hall.

"You realize," Anders said, "that you're the future, right?"

"And definitely not him," Jake added.

"We've all read at least a few fragments, and I've never seen anything like that in any of them," Tez said, turning to Kit and Finn.

"Me neither," Finn said, "and why is everybody going crazy over this guy all of a sudden? They used to say he was just fat, stupid, and lazy."

Kit nodded in agreement.

The crowd suddenly fell silent, and the five looked back toward to the stage.

Bigly paused for a moment to let the tension in the room rebuild.

"And one last thing," he shouted, "with everything that's going on right now—and with all the danger that lies ahead—from this moment on, I say no strangers should be welcome in our town! I mean, how can we trust any of them? How do we even know that they're not spies for the foxes? So I say to you, right here and now, no more strangers!"

Everyone cheered, and as if out of nowhere, they all started chanting, "No more strangers! No more strangers!"

The truth was that this hadn't just popped into Bigly's head on the spur of the moment—Dweezil had planted the idea into his feeble mind earlier that day.

Bigly let the rage build, nodding along with the chant.

As the mayhem climbed to a crescendo, he turned to Lanky, who was standing off to the side of the stage, and smiled his best smile ever.

Bigly knew he now had all these idiots in the palm of his hand and that they would follow him to hell and back.

They *were* lemmings after all.

"This is crazy!" Tez yelled, barely audible over the noise of the crowd.

"Just look at them," Jake said. "How can they believe any of his nonsense?"

"Well, they do," Finn said, "and I'm not sure there's anything any of us can do about it."

They all paused for a moment.

"Too bad Old Jobe isn't around," Jake said.

"You're right," Anders said. "From what I've heard, he'd put this lunatic back in his place."

"Who's he?" Finn asked.

"The stuff of legend," Anders said.

"Nobody's seen him for years. Keeps to himself now," Jake said.

"So he's still alive?" Tez asked. "Where is he?"

"Nobody knows," Anders said. "But even if he is alive, he must be very old by now."

There was another long pause, but this one was longer.

They turned back to the stage, and the crowd was getting crazier by the second. It was as if everybody in town had taken some kind of strange drug.

In truth, they had, and its name was Bigly. He had somehow managed to infect the community with stupidity. Everyone in Lemmingtown was now beyond being reasoned with. Facts no longer mattered, nor did modest and decent behavior. The culture of Lemmingtown had suddenly become one of catch words and slogans. It seemed that the entire community had simply given up thinking for themselves.

Bigly had long since stopped speaking, or rather ranting, as the mob carried on.

There he was, Bigly, standing center stage and basking in the glory and soaking in the energy of the crowd—eating it all up. It was as sustaining to him as some kind of magic elixir.

This was symbiosis in its purest form, and in a way, there was a perverse elegance to it. The crowd was Bigly's drug, and Bigly was theirs. It wasn't hard to imagine that this could quickly spin completely out of control—if it hadn't already.

The five of them turned back and looked at one another with expressions mixed with disbelief, shock, and horror.

"You're right, Jake," Anders said. "If only Old Jobe were here, Maybe he could get the town out of this mess."

"So where is he?" Tez shouted above the thunder.

"Like I said, nobody knows," Anders said.

There was another long pause, and then Kit said, "I do."

Six

(Tez's Search)

Kit knew? Everyone turned to her with their jaws hanging wide open.

"How?" Anders asked.

"Okay," Kit said, "I think I *might* know."

"What do you mean? You *might* know?" Anders asked again.

"How could you possibly know?" Jake asked as well.

"I don't know for sure, but if he's still alive, I think I might know how to figure out where he is."

"How?"

"I've never told this to anyone, but my family is directly descended from the Ancients."

Everyone fell silent, utterly dumbstruck by what Kit had just revealed.

"They lived a strict and disciplined life, and each generation taught the next. But their gift was only passed on to the firstborn. Firstborns were meant to carry some kind of torch to the future. Many, many generations ago, they were revered and referred to as *Legacies*. They were the embodiment of the Ancients. I believe Old Jobe may be the last of them."

"So how do you fit in?" Anders said.

"And how would you possibly know how to find him?" Jake added.

"Because my grandfather was a Legacy. He was the last in my family. He mentored Jobe when he was very young. Grandad's first daughter, my aunt, would have been next but died before she had any children."

"So doesn't that make you a Legacy?" Finn asked.

"No, it doesn't work that way," Kit said. "They're born with some kind of gift or something. Trust me. I may be related, but I'm no Legacy."

"So how could you know how to find him?" Anders asked.

"I'm only saying I *might* know," Kit said. "My uncle told me when I was very young that Jobe had left behind something important for me. It's supposed to be buried in my room somewhere, but I've never looked for it. Maybe it's a letter or something."

A strange feeling flooded over Tez, and she stood frozen for a second and then started to quiver. It was as if something had suddenly been awakened in her.

The others noticed that something decidedly odd was happening right in front of their eyes, and they all pulled back.

"Get me that letter," Tez said deliberately, with no inflection in her voice. "I *need* to see that letter!"

The group closed in around her. It wasn't frightening, but it was as if something had suddenly taken hold of her.

Kit bolted out of the hall, and the rest scurried after her. They zigzagged through the labyrinth of tunnels, with Tez following close behind.

Kit stopped short of her room. Everyone was completely out of breath, all except for Tez. Kit squeezed herself into her tiny room, and Tez followed her inside, while the others stayed behind and peered inside. They all held their ears up to the entrance to hear what was going on.

Kit started digging into the wall behind where she slept. There was nothing there at first, so she kept digging but still found nothing. The others watched on, wondering what she might find. She kept on digging and digging into other walls until she had clawed her room into total upheaval.

She looked over at Tez who somehow seemed to know exactly what she had to do. Tez rushed to the far corner of the room and started digging frantically into the floor, as if guided by some inaudible voice. She dug and dug but found nothing. She glanced behind her and saw Kit was now digging into the floor as well. A moment of self-doubt flashed through her mind, and she thought about digging somewhere else for a second, but she somehow knew she was right.

So she kept digging and digging and digging. Then with one final stroke of her flattened middle claw, she hit something.

Tez reeled back with a mixture of trepidation and awe, but she wasn't frightened by what she had unearthed.

"What is it?" Kit asked.

"What is it? What is it?" the others called from the entrance.

Tez summoned all her courage and peered into the hole again.

She spotted a tiny opening at the bottom of it. A strange feeling of calmness swept over her, and she began to feel warm inside and knew exactly what she had to do. She stood upright and plunged herself headlong into the hole, aimed straight at the tiny opening.

Kit rushed to the edge and looked in.

There was nothing.

The tiny opening had closed, and Tez was gone. She might as well have vanished into thin air right in front of her eyes.

Deep underground, after what seemed like an eternity, Tez crashed to the hard floor. Oddly enough, it hadn't hurt her in the slightest. She stood up and gave herself a shake. She was completely uninjured and feeling better than at any other time in her life. She felt as if she was being embraced by some kind of warm, protective blanket. She felt no fear nor any apprehension.

Tez glanced around and realized she had fallen into a labyrinth of tunnels unlike anything she had ever seen or could ever have imagined. But she also knew that many, if not most of them, might lead to some kind of trap or possibly something worse.

All the while, the calmness she had felt when she had first peered into the hole was growing pleasantly warmer. It was as if she was somehow being welcomed into this strange underground world.

She flicked her head around as she tried to decide where to go next. She spotted a faint blue glow coming from the end of one of the tunnels. Something about it called out *home* to her.

She instinctively rushed toward it, and just as she reached the entrance, the ceiling behind her began to collapse. She was shocked at first, but the glow grew brighter and more inviting as she scurried further into the tunnel. She could hear more and more of the tunnel collapsing behind her and moved faster. A moment later, she realized scurrying wasn't going to save her, so she started running as fast as she ever had in her life.

Everything began collapsing all around her, and the destruction was spreading by the second. Just then, she spotted three new tunnels up ahead. She had no time to choose, but she saw the same blue glow coming from the one in the center. She sped straight at it, but something deep down inside her told her to veer hard to the right.

That was exactly when the ground in front of the center tunnel collapsed, opening an enormous pit to her left. She scurried around the perimeter and threw herself headlong into the entrance to the center corridor. That was when everything behind her completely disintegrated, and the ground evaporated into a cloud of dust and utter destruction.

She collapsed to the floor, utterly exhausted.

She lay there, shaking, but still not frightened in the slightest. It took a moment to catch her breath before she sat up.

Her mind raced to comprehend what had just happened.

She sat still for a moment until, somewhere behind her, a calm and soothing voice spoke softly to her and said, "Do not be afraid, little one."

She collapsed back to the floor.

Tez slept for what seemed like an eternity.

Anyone else might have been concerned, but Jobe knew better. He checked on her often to make sure she was comfortable, squeezing twigs and bark underneath her so she wouldn't get cold, lying there on the bare floor of the cavern.

When she finally woke up, Jobe was standing over her again, gazing down and smiling a profoundly kind smile.

Total calmness swept across her, and she felt good.

"Hello again, little one. Welcome back," Jobe said in the same calm and reassuring voice she remembered from before.

"Hello," Tez said, completely at peace with everything she had just gone through, which now seemed like eons before.

"Where am I?" she asked softly.

"With a friend," Jobe said.

"Are you Old Jobe?" she asked again.

"What do you think?"

"I don't know. I'm just so tired."

"Yes, I understand. I felt that same way too, but it was a very long time ago."

"Where am I?" she asked once more.

"Where you belong," Jobe said. "And yes, I am Jobe. And I suppose I am old now, though I've never really thought about it that way before."

Tez looked up at him, and Jobe continued, "We are in a secret and sacred place built by the Ancients. Only you and I now have the privilege of knowing it. I believe we may be the last two."

"The last two? I don't understand."

"We are the last of the Legacies, and I think I know why you are here."

"But I'm not a Legacy. I'd never even heard of it until last night."

"I believe you have a special gift," Jobe said, "and I also believe that it is far greater than mine."

"Why?" she asked.

"Because I knew you and Kit when you were both very young, and it was her grandfather who mentored me. I also know that without you, Lemmingtown might have no chance of surviving."

"How could you know that?" she asked.

"Because I have spent most of my life here. This is where I have studied and protected the ancient texts, and I have always known this day would finally arrive."

"I thought they were just fragments," Tez said.

"That is only what everyone in the town believes. But I am, and have been, the guardian of the *actual* texts for a very long time now."

"May I see them?" Tez said.

"Of course, but I'll only show you where they are for now."

She got up, and Jobe led her through another labyrinth of tunnels and into a small chamber, just off to the left.

She was overwhelmed by the sight.

The hollow was bathed in the same blue glow that had guided her to Jobe. There was a small mound of stones piled in the middle of the room where three tablets lay. They seemed to be the source of the glow.

"Do they always look like that?" Tez asked.

"Look like what?"

"That light," she said, "the light that brought me here."

"Yes," Jobe said. "But only to you and I."

He paused for a moment then added, "I rather feel like taking a stroll right now. Join me, won't you?"

They meandered through more tunnels, and after one last turn to the right, there was a bright light at the end of what seemed like a giant cavern, and Tez was awestruck when they emerged.

The light was coming from a small passage that opened to a ledge that jutted out from an enormous rocky cliff.

It was brilliant and overwhelming, and there were thunderous crashes coming from waves colliding against the rocky shore far below.

The sun was just about to rise, and the view was breathtaking.

Jobe allowed a few moments to pass for Tez to soak it in.

They sat for a long time, gazing out over the huge expanse of water that merged into the distant horizon. No words were spoken, and Jobe's own memories began flooding back to him from the first time he had witnessed that same view so long ago.

Tez didn't know how much time had passed because time had now lost all meaning to her. It was as if time had begun moving more slowly—it was measured and deliberate and yet slipped by with complete ease.

Tez had never seen the sea before. Like most of the others in Lemmingtown, she had spent most of her days deep inside the tunnels, venturing outside only briefly to gather food a few times each day.

Jobe finally broke the silence in a calm and measured voice.

"What do you see?" he asked.

"It's wonderful. It's so beautiful. What is it?"

"It's called the ocean," Jobe said. "It's like a giant river."

This meant nothing to Tez, never having seen a river before.

"Are you frightened?" Jobe asked.

"No, not at all. I feel calm. Somehow I feel completely at peace. It's like nothing I've ever felt before," she said.

"I know," he said.

"How long have you been here?"

"A long time. A very long time, and I will explain it all to you one day. But we should eat now," he said.

Tez followed Jobe as he left the ledge and climbed out onto the rocky cliffs to search for food.

Seven

(The Conception of Lemming City)

Tez had been gone for days, but her friends had returned each day to the place in Kit's room where she had vanished. Everyone, that is, except for Kit. She had moved out that fateful night and now went to great lengths to avoid even passing by it—the mere thought of her old room haunted her.

There were mementos lying all around in the hopes she might miraculously return, but as the days turned to weeks, the visits became fewer and fewer until nobody entered the room again. Weeks turned to months, and Bigly finally seemed to have gained total control over the town. It wasn't through any conflict or struggle—it was only by the hypnotic power of his gatherings that never failed to persuade the crowd to believe in things that went completely against their best interests.

The stupidity of the mob had grown by the day. They loved all the excitement and spectacle of Bigly's events and loved being whipped up by his increasingly-outlandish commentary, claims, and catch phrases. They couldn't care less about what he actually had to say because they were too busy extracting the strange energy that came from being one of the believers. It was exactly the same kind of excitement as Bigly extracted from controlling them.

Bigly kept flashing his big stupid grins during every gathering, but he had also taken to scowling at anyone who dared question his plans. The scowls eventually turned into childish verbal assaults—he was Bigly after all.

Work on tunnels extending beyond Lemmingtown and out into the frontier continued at a feverish pace, and it wasn't long before they reached what would become *Lemming City*, as Bigly had already named it.

The construction eventually extended well beyond where any reasonable lemming would consider it to be safe. Furthermore, Lemming City was being built in great haste and without care. There was little thought put into any of the construction, quite simply because Bigly had little thought, and he had nothing but distain for anyone who would dare make any suggestion about how the project might be improved.

Bigly never visited the city, which he full well knew to be hazardous. Instead, he instructed his disciples to represent him. They all promised great rewards for any lemmings who would become one of the New Ancients, and volunteers were flocking in, especially right after every gathering, which had become almost daily events. Bigly never failed to whip the crowd into a frenzy that always climaxed with outlandish claims of what the future would hold if only they followed him.

None of it ever amounted to anything more than empty promises, some of which were so clearly impossible that even Bigly himself sometimes thought might have stretched too far. But none of it mattered in the slightest because the response from the crowd was always the same, chants of

"Bigly! Bigly! Bigly!" and "Outfoxed the foxes!" And that was all that really mattered to him.

Bigly began to spend most of his days indulging himself with overeating and increasingly-frequent visits from groups of attractive young females who were constantly summoned to his room. But above all else, his lust for adoration from *his* lemmings continued to grow by the day.

Nothing could stop him now!

As work continued on Lemming City, Bigly often thought of Mr. Sid and their deal, which had been constantly simmering in the back of his mind. He knew he had to start delivering on his promise of sending a seemingly-endless supply of food to a fox whom Bigly naively thought might become his best friend and ally one day.

Late one night Bigly dreamed about his second meeting with Mr. Sid and vividly remembered his luxurious quarters, with all the food and beautiful vixen that Mr. Sid surely always had at his disposal. *I might have outfoxed him*, Bigly thought, *but that doesn't mean I can't try to be a little more like Mr. Sid.*

He woke up early the next morning with a plan. He needed new quarters, and he needed them right away.

He sent for Dweezil and the rest of his inner circle, including Lanky, and they arrived at his room a little later. Dweezil led the way in, and all of them could tell in an instant that Bigly had worked himself into a lather. None of them were quite sure how to respond to it. Nobody, that is, except for Dweezil. He knew exactly what to do without missing a beat. He was going to stoke Bigly's mental fire by heaping praise on him.

"Good morning!" he said enthusiastically. "You were fantastic last night, sire!"

Bigly had never heard the term *sire* before and had no idea what it meant, but he very much liked the sound of it. He took it to mean he was a lemming of great importance, if not noble. He stuck his chest out, and paced around his confined room, ready to unveil his plans for new and luxurious accommodations.

"What a night I've had!" Bigly declared. "I have some amazing plans that we need to get started on without delay!"

"If you've had a marvelous night, sire," Dweezil said, "then we've all had marvelous nights."

"Yes, yes," Spencer said, "please tell us more, sir."

Spencer hadn't missed Bigly's reaction to Dweezil's use of the word *sire* and knew he could ingratiate himself further simply by adopting it, but it seemed a little much to him, so he chose *sir* instead. He even considered bowing a little, as a sign of obedience, but then thought better of it. Yes, he thought, groveling and loyalty were the keys to winning Bigly over forever, but he decided to save all that for later.

Derk and Saggy nodded wildly in agreement, adding "Tell us more!"

Bigly was bursting with pride and brimming with excitement. It was the same feeling he craved from the crowd, even though there were only five of them—the five sycophants.

"I've come to rely on each and every one of you," he said. "You are my trusted advisors. Never questioning and always able to see the brilliance of my plans. You are my crew, my team, my gang. What we need now is a new home base. You know, a big comfortable space. And by comfortable, I mean incredibly comfortable for me and, of course, for you as well. Make it huge! Think huge and make it even huger! Get some volunteers for this special project and get them right away. Make it happen. For me. For us. For the sake of the city!"

"Yes, sir!" they shouted, more or less in unison. They turned and scurried out of the room, but Bigly called out to Dweezil as they were leaving. Spencer glanced back, and a feeling of jealousy spilled over him.

Bigly spoke to Dweezil in hushed tones that conveyed tremendous seriousness and importance.

"As my most trusted advisor, I'd like it if you could take care of a certain matter that must be treated with the utmost delicacy. No, the utmost *secrecy*."

Dweezil could barely contain his excitement—he was about to be entrusted with a secret mission.

Bigly went on to outline his plans to construct a secret tunnel that extended far beyond Lemming City and even deeper into the frontier. It would serve as the launch pad for a series of expeditions into the wilderness. Eventually, as the city grew bigger and bigger under his direction, new volunteers could push out and establish satellite villages. Eventually, everything in between would be filled in, and Lemming City would become gigantic!

Dweezil was absolutely enthralled as Bigly outlined his plan, which was really nothing more than a means to begin fulfilling his promise to Mr. Sid.

"It's absolutely brilliant! Pure genius!" he said in a hushed voice. "You are truly the greatest and smartest and wisest of all lemmings."

Bigly didn't smile or even grin his stupid grin. He simply nodded in agreement, as if this was some well-established fact.

Bigly continued, "But first, we'll need to gather a secret squad of brave warriors, who will have to swear to complete secrecy. And of course, they must pledge complete loyalty to me and only to me."

"Understood," Dweezil said, nodding.

"And I think it would work best if they're not well known in town. You know, loners."

"Of course."

"Would you look after that for me?" Bigly asked.

"Absolutely!" Dweezil said. He started to scurry out of the room but turned back when he reached the doorway and added, "Thank you, sire!"

A single thought swept across Bigly's simple mind, and he broke out into the biggest and stupidest of his big stupid grins: *Yes, I am truly the greatest and wisest of lemmings.*

And with his renewed confidence, Bigly continued to spiral more and more out of control every day. He quickly became completely disconnected from reality and entirely divorced from any decent form of moral conduct.

He kept himself busy watching over Dweezil trying to enlist volunteers for dangerous missions deep into the frontier with flimsy promises of how they were true warriors and would be granted special status in the city. These lemmings were, of course, nothing more than sacrifices to Mr. Sid, and Bigly couldn't care less.

Weeks had gone by without any gatherings, and Bigly was craving adulation from his adoring crowd. He could also sense that his followers would now welcome another gathering as much as he needed one.

Bigly had sent for his inner circle, and when they arrived at his new headquarters, they entered a spacious receiving room. Lexie, a striking young female, escorted them into an elegant receiving room but not before they managed to sneak a glance into an opulent hall inside Bigly's expansive new quarters.

Each of them had become obsessed with how best to ingratiate themselves with Bigly. They had all grown suspicious of one another, and their jealousies began to consume a considerable amount of their attention. None of them would ever dare to mention it, least they'd be betrayed by another who might have had the better part of Bigly's ear at the moment. Bigly's favors flip-flopped throughout the course of each day, and Bigly knew how to play them well. He knew that they would compete for his attention forever, and he liked it that way.

Bigly thrived on the upheaval—it had all become a great game to him—admittedly not as satisfying as the cheering crowds during his gatherings, but the feeling he extracted from it had been enough to tide him over until his next performance.

He was adept at sowing seeds of distrust among his aides and disciples to keep them in a state of frenzied chaos. They all tried to outplease Bigly at one another's expense.

What luck, he thought, *that lemmings would rather follow than think.*

Lexie led Bigly into the room the moment after he had decided that his sycophants had waited just long enough to go overboard with lavish praise.

Of course, they didn't fail to deliver.

After a sufficient amount of gushing, Bigly interrupted them and said, "Please, please, let me bring you up to date on one of my biggest and most secret of plans."

The inner circle hushed themselves, and Bigly launched into his speech.

"You are my most trusted confidants and advisors. You are my lieutenants—no, let me rephrase that. You are my generals! And indeed, you are truly my dear friends. You may not be aware that I entrusted Dweezil with a mission of the utmost secrecy and importance, and the time has come, my generals, to finally share this great plan with all of you."

Although they were disappointed that something had happened behind their backs, they were all basking in their new titles. They were now *generals*, and they knew they were truly entrenched in something that would prove to be history in the making. They would be part of the movement that would transform Lemmingtown into the city of the future—Lemming City.

Bigly flashed one of his big stupid smiles. When the others all smiled back, Dweezil broke out into an enormous grin, possibly bigger and even more goofy than Bigly himself.

Bigly went on to share his secret plan for the satellite villages and how he was only able to share it with them now. He explained it to them in mock humble tones which the sycophants embraced with delight. He thanked them for their patience and understanding. Dweezil basked in all of it because he felt that Bigly was somehow praising him.

In truth, Bigly couldn't care less about Dweezil, or any of them for that matter.

Plans were made to prepare the biggest and greatest gathering ever. And after much discussion, which wasn't really a discussion at all, rather than a monologue from Bigly of what he more or less wanted to be done. As always, it was entirely devoid of details or any suggestions from Bigly about how to pull off this gargantuan event.

"One last thing. We need a name. A big beautiful name. A strong name. A powerful name. A name that conveys all the importance of what will be remembered as the biggest and greatest gathering in history . . ."

Bigly took a long pause then added, "Any ideas?"

All of the inner circle glanced at one another, each afraid to be the first to put anything forward, least it was immediately shot down by Bigly or, worse, ridiculed for even having been suggested it in the first place. Dweezil was clever enough to avoid offering up the first idea and stared at the rest of them with eyes like slits.

"How about we keep it simple? You know, call it what it is. Call it The Great Gathering," Derk offered.

Bigly nodded and said, "Hmmm . . . not bad. And at least it's direct."

"Greatest!" Spencer blurted out.

"Better," Bigly said.

"The Greatest Gathering Ever!" Saggy yelled out, to which Bigly nodded his approval.

Then each of them started belting out every adjective they could think of, like *gigantic, gargantuan, fantastic, amazing, epic, beautiful,* and so on.

Bigly really enjoyed watching each of them trying to outdo one another just to please him.

None of it even came close to the rush he felt from the gatherings, but he thought it not bad at all.

Dweezil had remained silent the whole time. He just watched and listened. Bigly turned to him and said, "We haven't heard anything from you yet. What do you think?"

Dweezil spoke calmly and said, "While all these may be excellent suggestions, in my mind, I keep landing on . . ."

"Yes . . .," Bigly said.

"The Huge Gathering," Dweezil offered cautiously but with an odd pronunciation of the word *huge* that sounded more like "uge."

The others looked at one another and then back at Dweezil. They all knew it was no better or worse than anything else that had been offered up.

All their eyes turned to Bigly. Lanky saw that Bigly might have liked it and yelled out, "Oh, I do like that one!"

"Then that's the one!" Bigly said, smiling at Lanky.

And as long as Bigly liked it, nothing else really mattered. Did it?

Eight

(The Education of Tez)

It was a week after Tez had arrived and adapted to Jobe's world that he began instructing her on the wisdom of the Ancients.

It all came naturally to her, but she also knew it was of the utmost importance, and she took her learning seriously, like some kind of solemn vow. She hung on every word Jobe had to say and learned quickly. Sometimes it was challenging, but more often it was as if she were merely being reminded of something that had been lurking in her subconscious her entire life.

Their days always began early, when the tunnels were still very dark. Tez never failed to sense when Jobe had awakened in his room down the hall, just past the room where the texts were held. She always waited patiently until she heard him pass by and then followed him through the maze of tunnels that led out to the cliffs. They sat there every morning and watched the sunrise. No words were exchanged—they just sat quietly, keeping their thoughts to themselves. They sat and absorbed all the splendor and majesty of the breaking dawn while waves crashed to the rocky shoreline far below. It would sometimes take hours before they got up and scrambled to the cliffside to tear away some moss shoots or other tender greens to eat.

One day Jobe finally broke the silence. It caught Tez a little off guard, but she wasn't really surprised at all. She always knew this day would finally arrive.

"The time has come," he said.

She knew that she was about to begin reading the texts, so she got up and followed him back through the tunnels toward the room with the blue glow. Jobe stopped at the entrance and paused for a moment of reflection.

They entered the room together, solemnly, without speaking a word.

The room grew gradually brighter with each step they took further inside until dozens of inscriptions were illuminated on the back wall along with scores of other tablets stacked in neat piles on the floor.

The large stack in the center of the room still seemed to be where the light was emanating from, but it was impossible for Tez to know with certainty.

The inscriptions were hieroglyphic and completely unintelligible to Tez. She glanced at Jobe. He simply nodded and said, "Soon you will understand some, but it will require a lifetime to understand them all. I continue to learn something each day, even after all these years."

Tez pored over the Ancient texts night and day. At first, she had needed guidance from Jobe, but it didn't take long before he left her on her own for many hours each day—but always after their silent observance of watching the sun rise each morning.

A day never passed when Tez didn't glean some new and profound insight into what the Ancients had been trying to establish so many generations before.

Every now and again, she would stop and sit silently, reflecting on the meaning of some passage and the insight she had just gained. There was much more to her learning than mere translation. It was a feeling of understanding and wisdom that somehow swept over her.

She continued to strip away at the memories of her ancient unconscious. Sometimes it felt to her like as if she was peeling open an onion, one layer at a time.

She fell asleep each night pleased and proud of what she had accomplished that day but always remained humble enough to know that she was only scratching the surface of a body of wisdom and knowledge that she might never be capable of fully understanding.

She persevered, and her learning continued for months.

Nine

(Lemming City Nears Completion)

Bigly had appointed Dweezil to take charge of planning the Huge Gathering, and he was perfectly suited for the job. He knew exactly what Bigly wanted, but it sometimes struck him as odd that no one else had ever really noticed it. Bigly wanted to be loved. But even more than that, he longed to be praised.

Dweezil's understanding of Bigly's motivations came easily to him because he shared the same insecurity as Bigly. He knew if he delivered a roaring success, Bigly might finally appreciate him at least a little the way he worshipped Bigly.

Dweezil also knew that anyone who would pretend to be some kind of king could easily be manipulated by dishing out an endless stream of compliments and flattery.

Bigly desperately needed to put on a spectacular show to feel loved again, and Dweezil intended to make the Huge Gathering Bigly's greatest performance ever.

Work on the construction of Lemming City had progressed at a remarkable rate, but it was still a long way from completion. Dweezil knew it would be premature to unveil Lemming City too early as there was still plenty of work to be done. He decided that Bigly should save the announcement of the completion of Lemming City until later and had spent hours coaching Bigly on exactly what he should and should not say at the Huge Gathering.

In truth, Lemming City hadn't really been much of a secret anyway because rumors of its remarkable progress had already been swirling, prompted by suggestions of Seamus and Carson and further fueled by leaks from Bigly's inner circle. Bigly had always pretended to be annoyed at the leaks, but he secretly loved it. It had kept the town abuzz and only added to the mystique of his uncanny ability to accomplish the impossible.

The evening of the Huge Gathering arrived, and the mob had already worked itself into a frenzy by the time Bigly and all his handlers finally arrived. He barely managed to reign in the uproarious crowd before he could launch into his most bombastic and ridiculous performance yet. It included all his greatest hits and went on for what seemed like forever.

Dweezil had been standing just off the side of the stage and was becoming intoxicated by how well Bigly's performance had been going. He tried to signal Bigly to wrap it up and even managed to catch Bigly's eye twice, but it was already too late. He knew Bigly just had to keep going on and on, like some runaway train.

Bigly, being Bigly, couldn't help himself and went completely off script, making everything up as he went along. It wasn't a conscious decision—it was just the way he was. So he told the town all about his wonderful city, Lemming City. He described its magnificence to them in great detail and how it was his gift to Lemmingtown.

Dweezil shook just his head and stared at the ground.

Bigly announced what he had already dubbed the *Grand Reveal* and that it was to be held the following week in Bigly Hall when Lemming City would finally be unveiled for all to see.

Even though Dweezil knew full well that this spontaneous act was premature and ill-advised, what did it matter, all the citizens of Lemmingtown were wildly keen to see this wonderful creation, and the Huge Gathering had been an enormous success, and that was all that mattered to Bigly and, therefore, to Dweezil as well.

Bigly basked in the glow from his announcement of the completion of Lemming City for days. The stupidity that Bigly had infected them with had become an entity unto itself. It was like a tidal surge that had become unstoppable.

Ten

(Return of the Legacies)

It was the day before the Grand Reveal when Tez and Jobe began their day as always. They had sat silently on the rocky cliff, staring out across the sea, focused only on the horizon, and completely lost in thought. Their routine was now well established. They would sit together until Jobe would stand and lead her out to the cliffs to collect some food for breakfast. He almost always sensed if Tez was following, but on some days he felt he had to glance back, just to be sure. Sometimes he would have to clear his throat gently to wake her from her contemplation. But this day was different, and for the first time, Jobe broke their silence abruptly.

"What are you thinking of, Young Tez?" he asked.

Tez was caught off guard, not only because Jobe had broken the silence, but also all the more because it was the first time he hadn't referred to her as *Little One*, and further, he somehow actually knew her by name, even though she had never mentioned it. But her surprise didn't last longer than a split second, and she displayed no physical sign of it at all.

"I was thinking about a passage I read yesterday. I read it over and over," she said. "Forgive me, but I can't quite recite it."

"That is quite all right," Jobe said softly. "What some consider to be knowledge is not really knowledge at all."

"What do you mean?" she asked.

"Quite often what seems to some as knowledge is nothing more than the mere recounting of words without understanding what was really meant by them."

Jobe paused, and Tez turned toward him.

"There is no reason to tell me *what* was written," Jobe said, "for I have read all the passages many times. Instead, tell me what it *said*. What did it say to you?"

"What I read made my fur stand on end. It was as if they had seen the future all those generations ago."

"Yes," Jobe said, "I know that feeling well. It is the feeling of insight and enlightenment. It's like discovering something, but it's also as if you had already known about it all your life."

"Yes," Tez said, "but how could the Ancients have known so long ago?"

"I know the passage you mean," Jobe said.

He stared off to the horizon and continued, "Days will surely come when many will lose their way and seek truth from those who know not where truth lies . . ."

He paused again and continued, "I fear that such a day may have finally arrived, and that is the reason why you are here."

Tez didn't respond. She simply stared back at Jobe, spellbound by his wisdom. He was like a prophet who knew what was about to happen—it was a gift she would someday inherit herself.

"We must go now," Jobe said.

"Where?"

"Why, back to Lemmingtown, Tez," Jobe said.

"Of course," she said.

Something inside of her clicked. She had transformed from Little One to Young Tez and had finally graduated to Tez. She was no longer a simple young lemming. She had become whom she had been destined to be all along. She had become *Tez*.

Later that day Tez followed Jobe as he scurried through the maze of tunnels that led to the cliff, but this time Jobe turned sharply to the left instead of taking the tunnel on the right that led outside.

Tez had noticed the tunnel before and had always wondered where it led but had never broken their silence to ask. She was about to find out. Up ahead, she could see that the tunnel rose, and she soon felt herself winding around a great spiraling section, climbing up and up.

After a lengthy climb, Jobe came to an abrupt stop just ahead of Tez.

"This part can be tricky. Follow my every step exactly," he said.

He pressed himself tightly against the left wall and crept forward carefully. Tez replicated his every step. Up ahead, the tunnel widened out, and Tez saw what looked like an enormous pit to her right. She pressed herself tighter against the wall, and a small piece of rock came loose under her right hind foot. She shuddered when the stone peeled off into what she could barely make out as some kind of abyss. There was no sound of it ever striking the bottom. Tez gulped.

Jobe sensed what had happened and called out, "Don't worry, you're doing fine," trying his best to comfort her while still keeping her focused.

"I sometimes wonder how many curious weasels have met their end here."

That was less comforting to Tez than he had intended.

"What's down there?" she asked nervously.

"It leads down to the rocks on the shore. The ones we can see from our ledge on the cliffs. It looks like a pretty rough landing from down below."

"So we're close to an exit then?" Tez asked again.

"Yes, we're close. Very close. You'll see it soon."

As they continued, the passage narrowed back into a tunnel again, and Tez breathed a sigh of relief with the pit now safely behind her. But her relief didn't last long. Further ahead, there was an incredible stench that somehow terrified her.

She began to tremble.

"What's going on?" she asked.

"Just another trick of the Ancients," Jobe said, half chuckling. "The first time I smelled it, I actually threw up, so you're ahead of me so far. Don't worry about it, you'll get used to it."

"What is it?"

"Wolf pee," Jobe said, "but none of the predators care for it either, especially the foxes."

"It's awful."

"Well, in a minute, we're going to rub ourselves in it."

"What?"

"It's how we're going to make it to Lemmingtown in one piece," Jobe said.

They stopped just short of what would turn out to be the entrance to the outside world and rubbed themselves against the wall. Jobe had been right. Tez was beginning to get used to foul smell, even though it still sickened her. She managed to keep her nausea at bay by reminding herself over and over how this stink was going to keep her alive.

Jobe crouched down and moved slowly toward a thick mass of dried vegetation. He poked his stubby nose into it, then pushed his way a little further inside, and paused. Tez followed him into the scrub.

This starting and stopping continued for a short time. Suddenly, with one last push, he broke through it, and they were flooded with brilliant light, completely outside.

They rushed behind some nearby rocks and hid for a moment.

Jobe held his nose up and sniffed over and over, flicking his head about quickly in every direction. He turned back to Tez and said, "I think we're okay."

Jobe nodded to the left and said, "Lemmingtown is over there, but we're going to head that that way," nodding to the right.

"Why?" she asked.

"We want to be upwind, so predators can smell us coming."

"What?"

"We're wolves, remember?"

"Oh right," she said.

They didn't have all that far to travel, but it was far enough and easily the most dangerous journey of Tez's life. Along the way, they spotted a couple of young foxes who were curious at first, only to race away once they caught scent of the pair.

The journey passed largely without incident, except for one terrifying moment when Jobe spotted a sinister-looking shadow streak across their path then pass back again. In a flash, Jobe shoved Tez into the rocks and under a heap of decomposing leaves and dove in after her.

"What is it?" she said.

"Predator," he said. "Up in the sky. Maybe a hawk. Probably an owl. It can't spot us under here and should move along after a time."

It was Angel, the snowy owl, who had been circling around on the hunt for a meal after a meager dinner the night before. They waited and waited, peeking out of the leaves occasionally, until the shadow hadn't streaked by for some time.

"We best get moving along before our disguise wears off."

They started to run, moving as fast as they could, darting in and out among the rocks and through the trees. Tez was sure she could hear some foxes yelping not far away, and her heart was pounding. Off to her left, she caught a glimpse of what looked like a group of lemmings being devoured, which made her run all the faster. Further ahead, they zoomed past a hidden entrance to Lemmingtown that Tez recognized, but she knew better than stopping to point it out—she trusted Jobe with her life and was certain he knew exactly what he was doing.

Jobe veered to his left and dove into a thicket of thorny bushes, crouched low to the ground. Tez followed close behind. Not far inside the brush, they crawled into a small hollow at the base of one of the bushes and stopped to catch their breath. They were panting heavily.

"We're here," he said cheerfully.

"Where?"

"An entrance that you're now the only other to know about," Jobe said.

"You saw the one back there, right?" Tez clarified.

"Of course."

"Why didn't we go in?" Tez said.

"Because there is something in here that I want to share with you," he said. "Follow me."

Jobe pressed himself into a narrow crack between some rocks with great difficulty, and Tez followed. It was dark and damp and cold and a little wet, but the moisture made it easier to slip further into the crack. Tez was following close behind Jobe when he suddenly disappeared from sight. She gasped. Then with one more difficult push through an even tighter split in the rock, she popped out into another world.

It was like some long-abandoned relic, filled with tunnels leading off in all directions. Although there was scarcely any light, there was just enough for Tez to barely make out dozens of markings on the walls after her eyes had adjusted. They looked similar to the writing in the texts, but different somehow.

"What is this place?" she asked.

"This is special place," Jobe said. "A marvelous place that must have been lost long ago. I discovered it not long before you arrived, and the timing now strikes me as curious."

"How did you find it? I mean, it wasn't exactly easy to get here."

"I know, and that's the point. I found it a little by accident but more by listening to what the texts were trying to tell me. One day it came to me. The texts don't describe it, but a passage I have read many times strikes me as guidance for where future generations could live."

"Who lived here?"

"I don't think anyone ever did."

"What's it for then?" Tez asked.

Jobe paused for what seemed like a long time while he collected his thoughts.

"I think it was intended as some kind of safe place. It may well have been intended to provide safe harbor for the citizens of Lemmingtown in a time of crisis. Well, some of them anyway."

He paused again and drew a long contemplative breath.

"I fear that day is coming and is the reason why we are here now. Did you notice all those lemmings being devoured by foxes as we ran past?"

"Yes! Yes, I did!" she said. "But I was too busy running for my life to mention it."

Jobe paused again and turned directly toward her. "What do you suppose they were doing all the way out there?"

"Strange, isn't it?" Tez said.

"Yes, it is, and I think I might know why, but we'll be safe here, and I think it's time to rest."

Eleven

(Two Worlds Collide)

Lemmingtown was abuzz the next morning. Everyone was still reeling from Bigly's announcement at the Huge Gathering and anxious to see Lemming City that evening.

Not far away, but what was really a world away, Jobe and Tez had slept through the night and awakened early to explore the tunnels and to wherever it was that they might lead. Jobe wasn't entirely sure, but he suspected they were situated somewhere above Lemmingtown. That made sense to him because it seemed natural that the Ancients might have built some kind of safe harbor, where they could retreat in the event of some unforeseen threat. He was pretty confident there'd be no traps or anything of that sort if this was, indeed, meant to be a safe place. But then again, the Ancients always seemed to have had more than a few tricks up their sleeves, so he made the conscious decision to never let his guard down.

The tunnels turned out to be a confounding labyrinth that kept circling back on one another. Tez and Jobe often took separate forks, but they always called out to each other to make sure neither of them became hopelessly lost. It was frustrating because they always ended up at exactly the same place where they had started from. They spent the better part of the morning exploring in vain, and it was only until midday that they decided to head out together to venture further afield.

They came to hub that split into a handful of other branches. Jobe started to lead her in one direction, but Tez stopped him.

"No," she said. "That's the wrong way. That way's a trap!"

Jobe turned to her with a knowing look on his face. Tez had graduated. He was now convinced she was *the* Legacy, the embodiment of all the Ancients from so long ago. He wasn't surprised by her taking charge, for he knew what she was feeling. He had felt it himself a very long time ago. From this point on, Tez would lead, and he would follow, just as his Legacy had been passed along to him so long before. And although she didn't realize it, the future of Lemmingtown was now resting on her shoulders.

"This way," she said and headed straight toward the second entrance from the right. It was a strange tunnel, fashioned into a switchback which disguised the fact that it was sloping downward. Every so often, there were entrances to other tunnels and sometimes forks in the road, but Tez remained undeterred. She bobbed and weaved her way through the tunnels until they came to an impasse—a giant mound of broken rock.

They stopped and turned to each other.

"I was sure this had to be the right way," Tez said, "but I'm not so sure now."

"Yes, you *believe* it is the right way, but I *know* it is," Jobe replied. "And I also know that very soon you too will turn your beliefs into knowledge."

"I don't understand," Tez said.

"Real knowledge comes from always testing your own beliefs and admitting when you are wrong. You can always adjust what you believe, but when you attain true knowledge, it will last forever. Look at what you see. Study it objectively. Thoughtfully. Step back and observe."

Tez took a few steps back and carefully surveyed the huge mound of rock, and for reasons she couldn't understand, she felt compelled to keep looking. She knew Jobe was trying to teach her something profound, but she still saw nothing. She grew more determined than ever. She stared intently at it again and studied the pile even more carefully. Every single rock and every single crevice.

And suddenly, there it was!

High up at the top of the heap, there was the tiniest hint of light just where the slope of the mound met the ceiling. What would have been imperceptible to anyone else now shone out like a beacon to Tez.

"How did you know it was there?" Tez asked.

"I didn't," Jobe said. "But I knew you would find it."

"Do you see it now?" she asked again.

"No. My eyes are too old and weak."

Tez paused to think as Jobe continued.

"Sometimes finding something depends on who's looking for it, and what they're looking for. And sometimes it depends on the reason why they're looking for it in the first place."

"But you had to tell me to look."

"Yes," Jobe said, "but now you are *observing*—not just merely glancing with fleeting looks as all the rest do."

Tez clambered up the mound towards the faint light. She stopped and stretched to peak through the tiny crack above her.

What she saw made her reel back. It was Kit's room—the same room where she had first fallen into the tunnels on that fateful night which seemed like a thousand years before.

"Good to be back?" Jobe asked.

Tez was unable to respond.

"This is the . . ."

"I know," Jobe said, "the room where your journey began, and you have now come full circle. Only the Ancients could possibly know what your destiny holds in store for you now."

Not far away, it was ten minutes before showtime at the Grand Reveal, and Bigly had polished himself up better than ever before—or at least as well as a fat lemming possibly could. His coat had been carefully coiffed, and Dweezil figured that Lanky probably had helped it, and he felt a pang of jealous envy.

Dweezil had already assembled a large entourage. There were sentries up ahead and to the sides, while he and the rest of the inner circle trailed directly behind Bigly. He had also added a cast of striking young female lemmings, gushing with delight for having been included in the spectacle. They too had all fallen under Bigly's spell, and each of them had their own plan on how best to ingratiate themselves with Bigly after the Grand Reveal.

Bigly and his entourage had left his quarters a few minutes after the gathering was supposed to have begun in yet another of his calculated theatrical entrances. As they wound through the tunnels toward the Great Room in Lemming City, even Bigly couldn't believe his own ears and eyes. There were throngs of lemmings absolutely packed into the tunnels outside the entrance to the grand and gaudy Bigly Hall, and the atmosphere was brimming with frenzied excitement.

The crowd fell silent as the procession approached, parting ahead of them that made it look like a ship slipping through fog on a glassy sea. There were a few cries, but most remained silent, stretching out a hand that they might exchange a touch or some other acknowledgment from Bigly, like a wink or a nod.

As they drew closer to the entrance to Bigly Hall, they heard an enormous noise spilling out of the cavern. It fell absolutely silent when they entered and stayed that way for long enough for Dweezil to start worrying what could possibly have gone wrong to prompt the silence.

Suddenly, Bigly Hall exploded into an absolute cacophony. The drug had been administered to the crowd at last, and its effects were immediate—and this time more potent than ever before.

Just behind the wall in Kit's room, Tez and Jobe scraped away at the rocks around the tiny slit so that it was just wide enough for them to squeeze through. Tez paused as she was just about to push herself out of the narrow hole and peered through. Her eyes darted around the room, and she remembered it like it was yesterday. Her eyes swung to the small entrance, and she saw hundreds of lemmings streaming past the doorway.

Lemmingtown was on the move.

Tez and Jobe managed to pry themselves through the fissure and into the room after the throng had passed. Tez was overwhelmed by what was obviously some kind of tribute to her, although she also noticed that had long been neglected. *Had it really been that long ago?* she thought.

"What do you think is happening?" Tez asked.

"I fear Lemmingtown is in imminent danger."

Tez took off without saying a word and squeezed herself out of the room while Jobe followed behind.

They weaved their way through the maze of tunnels, always careful to navigate around the traps in a way that still came as second nature to Tez, although Jobe had long forgotten the route.

They ran hard and fast until they closed in on the throng that had passed by.

Right there, at the back of the pack, Tez spotted her friends—keeping themselves at a distance from the masses as they always had done since the beginning of Bigly's reign.

Tez called out, and Kit recognized her voice in an instant. Kit screeched to a halt and turned back.

"Tez!" she shrieked. "We thought you were gone!"

"We thought you were dead!" Anders shouted.

"Well, I'm here and definitely not dead."

Jobe had fallen a little behind but pulled up next to Tez, panting heavily.

"Let me introduce you to somebody special," Tez said. "This . . . this is Jobe."

Everyone was awestruck. They circled around the pair and stood in silence while they tried to digest all of what had just happened.

So this was Old Jobe, the legend. He looked exactly like any of them would have expected. He was distinguished with a reassuring glint of wisdom in his eyes. He was like a kindly grandfather who cared for everyone else and very little for himself. Old Jobe was the embodiment of all the virtuous character that Bigly would never be capable of ever understanding, let alone acting on.

"What's happening? Where is everyone going?" Tez asked, breaking the stunned silence.

Tez's friends were still reeling from her sudden return, not to mention finally meeting Old Jobe.

"What do you mean what's happening?" Anders asked back. "What happened to you?"

"Where did you go?" Jake also wanted to know.

"There will be plenty of time for that later," Jobe said in a serene voice. "It would seem something of great significance is about to take place."

"Where's everyone going?" Tez asked again.

"A lot has happened since you vanished down that hole," Kit said.

"They're all heading to Lemming City," Anders added.

"Lemming City?" Jobe asked.

"Yes, Bigly has transformed Lemmingtown into a city that extends far into the frontier." Finn said.

Tez and Jobe glanced at each other, now understanding why they had seen all those lemmings being eaten by foxes out in the wilderness so far from Lemmingtown.

"You mean that great, fat, lazy lump who claims to have outfoxed the foxes?" Tez said.

"Everybody seems to have fallen in love with him," Kit said. "It's as if they're all under some kind of spell."

"How could they be so gullible?" Tez said.

"Well, not exactly everybody," Anders added. "We think he's mad, but everybody else is willing to do anything he says, no matter how crazy it sounds."

"So who is taking care of Lemmingtown?" Jobe asked.

"Just us," Kit said, "and a handful of others."

"Oh my," Jobe said.

Tez and Jobe glanced at each other again, and Tez's fur stood up on end as a chill swept across her.

"So why was this city built in the first place?" Tez asked.

"Because the population of Lemmingtown has exploded," Anders said.

They had suddenly realized exactly what was happening. Everyone, well almost everyone, had forsaken all that Lemmingtown had stood for. It had been established with so much thought and care and struggle. It had been a marvelous town that was safe and secure and provided the perfect home for so many lemmings and for so many generations. It struck them that all this had suddenly been tossed away.

"I suggest we discuss this later," Jobe said. "We need to follow them and see this Lemming City for ourselves," Jobe said.

Twelve

(The Grand Reveal)

Kit led the way through the last of the ancient tunnels of Lemmingtown, with Tez following close behind. It reminded her of the fateful night that Tez had disappeared so long ago. Jobe hung back a little to better see how Tez would handle herself.

When they reached the edge of Lemming City, they saw an entrance with an enormous inscription above it that proudly proclaimed, "Welcome to Lemming City."

From what Jobe had already heard about Bigly, he wondered for a moment why it hadn't already been named *Bigly City*. But sure enough, when they passed into the new tunnel, slogans paying homage to Bigly were plastered all over the walls in a most untactful manner. It looked like graffiti on the side of an abandoned warehouse.

Bigly City!
Outfoxed the foxes!
Bigly Forever!

As they scurried further into the tunnel, comments like *moron*, *pathetic*, and *loser* percolated through the group of skeptics.

Most of the tributes had probably been at the direction of Bigly himself as the majority had been struck into the walls in a strikingly-similar style. It was obvious that all these staged tributes were nothing more than manufactured self-adulation and clearly the work of a profoundly-insecure and troubled mind.

The group scurried further down the tunnel to catch up with Bigly's followers. They passed by large empty caverns, which had obviously been excavated with great labor, but served no clear purpose.

The further they continued inside, the more apparent it became that the whole project was a disastrous mess. The construction was slipshod, and there were absolutely no defenses at all—not even some half-baked attempts to give the appearance of protecting this new city. It would have been laughable if it hadn't posed such a serious existential threat to Lemmingtown.

Lemmingtown had grown over years of patient care, but Lemming City was nothing but a showy, slap-dash mess. And all the slogans proved to be right. This monstrosity truly deserved to be renamed *Bigly City*. Or perhaps *Bigly's City* would have described it better. Its flawed nature was nothing but a manifestation of its flawed creator.

By the time the group had caught up with the rest of the town, Tez could feel the electricity of the mob in the air—the tunnel was packed with sweaty lemmings, all jostling and pushing their way into the grand theatre that lay ahead.

Any semblance of cooperation or any kind of the polite and courteous behavior that had been the mainstay of life in Lemmingtown would never have any place in Lemming City.

Jobe stared at Tez with disbelief in his eyes. Tez, who had already witnessed one of Bigly's gatherings, was even more shocked. The situation had grown more dire than she could have ever imagined.

The crowded tunnel eventually emptied out as everyone finally pushed their way through the entrance and into Bigly Hall.

Kit, Tez, Jobe, and the rest were the last to enter and managed to push their way to the back of Bigly Hall.

The sheer size of the cavern was overwhelming. Even Tez had to concede that it was impressive—at least to look at for the first time. It was glitzy and showy but clearly hastily assembled and in an instant, would strike any sensible lemming—at least any lemming who tried to govern themselves in accordance with the ways of the Ancients—as gaudy and superficial and completely lacking in substance. It had all the hallmarks of its creator.

The gathering was about to get underway as they reached the back of the hall.

Lemmings just ahead of them occasionally glanced back to see who was behind them. There was a stir in the crowd as more and more turned their heads back. Some were staring. Jobe spotted an old lemming, whom he vaguely recognized, and offered a respectful nod.

A different kind of excitement had been building at the front of the hall as Bigly started off on with another predictable rant about how great Lemming City was and how the citizens of Lemmingtown were all indebted to him.

That was when the trouble began.

Bigly was going on and on, in his usual confused and rambling way, about how they needed more recruits to venture out into the frontier and how anyone who would help extend Lemming City would go down in history as one of the greatest of the New Ancients.

The hall was drowning with all the usual chants of "Bigly, Bigly, Bigly!" and everything else that had become commonplace. All decorum and what would have been considered societal norms in Lemmingtown had been completely abandoned.

None of this would have been surprising to any outside observer. Bigly was a drug, and he craved the adulation of the masses as much they craved him.

Bigly hadn't outfoxed the foxes. He had merely conned the residents of Lemmingtown—well, most of them anyway.

Bigly's onstage rant continued.

"We owe a tremendous debt to all our New Ancients!" he yelled.

It was met with thunderous cheers and applause. Bigly may have been fat and stupid and lazy, but his remarkable gift for manipulating a crowd like puppets on strings continued to grow by the day.

"And this is why I know so many more of you will step forward and rise to the occasion!"

He took a long dramatic pause and then declared, "As you can see for yourselves, Lemming City is already great, and I will make it even greater! For I am Bigly!"

The crowd went hysterical and someone yelled out, "You are the chosen one!"

How perfect was that for Bigly? The mob was writing its own material. They had graduated. They were feeding themselves. It was new. It was fresh. It was exciting. It was chants of "Cho-sen one! Cho-sen one! Cho-sen one!"

Bigly stepped back and nodded along spasmodically to the rhythm of the frenetic chanting.

But the adoration was not universal. And just as the chants were fading away to give Bigly a chance to continue ranting, somebody at the back of the room called out, "Who chose you?"

Bigly had seemed to have tricked nearly every lemming in Lemmingtown with his lies and manufactured phony persona—but not everybody. Although some might have thought it before, they had been too caught up with all of Bigly's showmanship to pay any attention to reason, let alone speaking out against his nonsense.

This one voice stood alone.

It was the voice of reason.

It was the voice of Tez.

Jobe turned his head toward her and smiled, for he knew that this single spark of insight, delivered by one strong voice, might be all that was needed to save the soul of Lemmingtown. She had sown a seed of doubt by simply questioning an otherwise arbitrary authority and holding it accountable.

Bigly had managed to seize control over Lemmingtown, not through some violent revolution or coup but merely by convincing most of the citizens of Lemmingtown that he could somehow make their existence better in some vague, never-to-be-spelled-out way. Leave it all to Bigly and you'll all be far better off—just trust him.

Bigly's greatest fear was being exposed for the fraud he was. He craved all the attention and adulation that he had created for himself out of thin air, with nothing more than lies, deceit, and false bravado. He had reinvented himself and grown into the role of playing *Bigly*. After all, he had outfoxed the foxes, hadn't he?

Like a consummate actor, he was no longer the fat and lazy Bigly of old. He had completely metamorphosed into the *character* Bigly and now actually believed his manufactured reality as much as any other Bigly worshiper. And it was on that day that he had truly and finally become Bigly. Bigly the chosen one!

Bigly's unconscious fears had grown so all-consuming that what would have been debilitating for most other lemmings had turned into his greatest strength. All the stress and anxiety had actually grown into Bigly's real power. It was even stronger than his uncanny ability to spin lies and talk his way out of anything.

But that single question from the back of the crowd had sent a shiver up his spine because it posed an existential threat to Bigly, the chosen one.

Bigly took a break from praising the New Ancient recruits for a moment to send for Dweezil and the other sycophants and send them out to confront this dissident at the back of the hall and shut them down. He wanted to be as ruthless as Mr. Sid and didn't mind if it even meant inciting violence.

Bigly had overestimated the extent of the loyalty of his supporters simply because he had always assumed that everybody else was as lazy as he was. He was surprised, even delighted, when Dweezil and the others arrived before the messenger had been dispatched.

"Sire!" Dweezil said. "The disturbance at the back of the hall is continuing and seems to be gaining support."

"How dare they!" Bigly shouted.

"Sire," Dweezil said, "we would be obliged if we could take care of this matter on our own, with your permission, of course."

"Permission granted," Bigly barked.

They turned and dutifully headed toward the back of the hall.

"Wait!" Bigly called out.

They turned back, worried that they might have offended him in some way.

"Thank you for your loyalty! And thank you for your resourcefulness!"

This was yet another example of Bigly's innate ability to manipulate others.

It was a gift that required no effort on his part, and it was something that he would never understand and sadly never employ it for any higher purpose. And even if he ever did, he could never appreciate this gift for what it was. He instinctively knew that by praising his disciples in front of these new recruits would be like an investment that would yield enormous dividends down the road.

Bigly went back to congratulating his new recruits as the five sycophants made their way to the back of the hall, pushing their way through the crowd.

When they arrived, the group surrounding Tez, Jobe, and her friends had swollen, and Dweezil could sense the threat that these nonconformists would pose if their views were allowed to spread any further.

Tez and Jobe had an otherworldly aura about them, and the crowd was mesmerized.

Tez had vanished and had been long given up for dead. But there she was, standing with Old Jobe, the legend, right in front of their own eyes and stealing the show right out of Bigly's hands.

Everyone was thinking it, but nobody was saying it: Maybe *they* were the real *chosen ones*. They were genuine, and there was no flash nor any pompous theatrics. They were exactly what many of the inhabitants of Lemmingtown needed after many months of craziness.

At the other end of the hall, Bigly was still ranting about how great Lemming City had already become and how much greater it was destined to be and how much of a debt everyone owed him for the fifth time. For he and only he, the chosen one, was the only means by which any of this could have been accomplished in such a short time.

The crowd was still chanting and cheering and gushing with adoration. It bordered on worship of this pathetically incompetent pretense of a leader. He wanted to be the first *ruler* in the history of Lemmingtown. It was an idea that the Ancients would have completely abhorred.

The group surrounding Tez and Jobe was abuzz with debate and revelation as Dweezil and the other sycophants pushed their way through the crowd. It was remarkable how quickly the seeds of doubt about Bigly had already begun to blossom into genuine dissension.

Dweezil had passed through the crowd with no signs of a struggle. It was as if a small part of them still felt Bigly deserved some kind of polite respect, even though they had never embraced him as everyone else in Lemmingtown had done. These Lemmings were decent, perhaps to a fault, and would never imagine putting up any kind of a fight.

"Tez has told me," Jobe said, "of what was happening in Lemmingtown, and I must tell you that I was concerned at first by what she told me."

The group was quiet, and even Dweezil paused to listen.

"But now that I see it for myself and after hearing from its creator . . ."

Jobe took a long pause. Not because he was using it as some dramatic prop, but rather because he was carefully trying to find the right words to describe the dismay that he truly felt.

Dweezil felt a brief moment of excitement because he actually believed that Jobe might have been impressed and was about to heap praises on Bigly.

"I am absolutely appalled," Jobe said. "This place, this Lemming City, is not the future of Lemmingtown, and it will mark its demise. This is the beginning of the end of your home. Our home. Our sanctuary and our entire way of life. Lemming City will perish when the last of its inhabitants are devoured by foxes and weasels. And it truly breaks my heart. How could you have possibly let this happen?"

"Liar!" Dweezil yelled out. "Lemming City is great!"

"And the best is yet to come!" Lanky added.

Everyone in the crowd around Tez and Jobe turned toward Dweezil, completely unfazed and still silent. It didn't outrage anyone in the group, and it was not provocative to them in the slightest. It merely displayed Dweezil for what he was—the puppet of a self-absorbed clown. The silent response crushed him. It was like a reaction to a bad joke after it falls flat.

Dweezil's show was over, and they all simply turned back toward Tez and Jobe. There was not going to be any fuss or confrontation here, and the lack of any sign of an agitated response deflated Dweezil even further.

Dweezil had no idea what lay in store for him as Tez retuned to center stage.

"What makes it great?" she asked.

"It is great because it was created from Bigly's vision, and he is the greatest lemming ever!" Dweezil replied.

"And what is it that makes Bigly great?"

"Bigly is great because he is a genius who outfoxed the foxes."

"Outfoxing the foxes would certainly make one clever, but how would it make one great?"

"Bigly is great, and everyone knows it! He is the chosen one!" Dweezil said, now growing increasingly agitated.

"Once again, who chose him?"

"We did! We all did!"

"No. Not everyone," Tez said.

"None of us did!" Kit added.

"Then you are nothing but fools!"

"So Bigly is great because he outfoxed the foxes?"

"Yes!"

"How do you know he outfoxed the foxes?" Tez asked.

"Because I was there!"

"How did he do it?"

Dweezil wasn't the sharpest lemming in town—although he did excel at conniving—but he was smart enough to realize he wasn't making things any better. And he knew the growing skepticism could be disastrous for Bigly if it continued unchecked. He knew what had to be done.

"I'll prove it to you!" he said. "I will bring Bigly himself back here to address all of you, and you will see for yourselves how truly great he is!"

Jobe, who had remained silent, finally spoke up and said, "I, for one, would very much look forward to hearing from this chosen one himself, instead of his messenger."

Dweezil's gang turned to head out, but before he led them back to Bigly, he paused and yelled, "Just wait and you will see all of Bigly's greatness for yourselves!"

With that, Dweezil led the other sycophants away, pushing through the crowd to the front of the hall where Bigly was still rambling on. They came around the stage from behind and waited off to one side as Bigly was wrapping up the Grand Reveal.

Bigly left the stage to thunderous cheers and chants and approached Dweezil.

"Well," he said, "did you pull those dissenters into line?"

"Not exactly, I'm afraid."

Bigly didn't say a word. He just scowled at them, and the rage in his eyes spoke volumes.

"They're very good at twisting words and spreading lies," Dweezil said nervously. "And they've even started sowing doubts among your followers about how great you truly are."

"Then I have no choice!" Bigly shouted.

Dweezil shuddered, worrying he might have finally fallen out of Bigly's favor, which had always been his greatest fear.

"You did the right thing in coming to me with this. You spotted a problem that only I can solve, and I will just have to look after it myself. Take me to them!"

Dweezil breathed a sigh of relief.

Bigly, on the other hand, was terrified. These sounded like smart lemmings, very smart lemmings, and there was nothing that scared him more than smart lemmings. He didn't know how to argue. He didn't know how to debate, and he had always been afraid for being exposed for the fraud he was.

He became momentarily paralyzed with feelings of insecurity and self-doubt. But he told himself that negative thoughts were for losers. And he was a winner! In an instant, he somehow managed to transform himself back into Bigly, the character, yet again. His resilience was uncanny. The only way to explain it was that he truly believed all the lies and crazy talk that he had been spouting while suppressing the real reason behind Lemming City in the first place.

The inner Bigly was undoubtedly the character Bigly's greatest fan.

Bigly and his entourage made their way to the back of the Great Hall led by strapping young male lemmings and accompanied, as always, by beautiful young females following along in tow. Seamus and Carson were right behind them, whipping up Bigly's most ardent supporters along the way with unfounded claims and crazy conspiracy theories.

Jobe was surprised that Bigly had taken on the challenge of trying to convince the growing crowd of skeptics around Tez and himself that he was the chosen one and not the fool that Jobe knew him to be.

Bigly made his way forward to confront Tez and Jobe.

"Bigly hears that you don't like what Bigly is doing and disrespect how great Lemming City has become."

Jobe and Tez looked at each other, wondering why Bigly was referring to himself in the third person. But it didn't take more than a second for them to connect the dots.

This puffed-up creature that stood before them was nothing more than a pathetic cartoon character—albeit a convincing one—who had conned Lemmingtown into believing he was something that he was not.

"What makes it great?" Tez said.

"Just look around! Only a fool could not see how truly marvelous my creation is!"

"Sure, it might look fine," Tez said.

"What do you mean *might* look fine?" Bigly interrupted. "It is fantastic, and it makes Lemmingtown look like a dump."

"As I was saying, while it might look fine, how long did it take to build?"

"No time at all!"

"So it was built in haste?"

"Record time! And only I could have built this big beautiful city so quickly!"

"So again, built in haste?"

"Of course! Weren't you listening? We accomplished all this in record time!"

Tez paused for a moment and looked around. It was showy and pretentious and had clearly been constructed with little skill or care. It was like a pretty cake that tasted bad.

"Who built it?" Tez questioned.

"We had all the best lemmings working on it. There was no end of volunteers, and more are joining us every single day. They are all true heroes!"

"So all your supporters then?"

"Exactly! They are the New Ancients, and they share my vision! Lemming City is great, and we are making history! I am making history!"

Tez paused for a moment to digest the magnitude of Bigly's hubris.

Snickers broke out in the group that had now circled around Bigly and Tez.

Bigly tried to brush it off and said, "See, they're all laughing at you."

The lemmings laughed even louder, and Bigly joined in as well, convinced he must have come up with some witty joke.

"Do any of these New Ancients have any experience in building?" Tez asked.

"Excuse me! Excuse me! That's a very rude question," Bigly said, "and you are a very rude lemming!"

Unlike the Bigly supporters at the front of the hall, the crowd at the back remained silent. Jobe turned toward Tez, curious how she would respond to this frivolous attack.

Tez simply said, "It's not a rude question. I'm just curious if anyone who built Lemming City has any experience or if all this is the work of some master builder who had merely employed the labor of others to complete their vision."

Jobe knew that Tez could read this pathetic idiot like a book, and a wry smile spread across his face.

"I built this city!" Bigly proclaimed.

"So you have the experience then?"

"I accomplished all this in record time! No other lemming could have done what I have done!"

"So you have experience then?" Tez repeated.

Bigly paused for a moment to figure out a way of moving off this unfortunate topic.

"You know," he said calmly, "when work started here, not so very long ago, a lot of lemmings came to me and said, 'How can you possibly know all this? How can you know how to build such a great city?'"

"That's a good question," Tez said. "How did you?"

"It comes from inside me," Bigly said. "It is a gift."

"Is it safe?" Tez asked.

"This is the safest city ever built!"

"Well, you've done a good job at hiding all the traps and tight turns in the tunnels that led us here."

"What do you mean by that?" Bigly demanded.

"It just doesn't look very safe to me."

"How dare you!"

"Where are all the sentries hiding?"

"We don't need any," Bigly said confidently. "All our security is above us, and it's the best known to any lemming anywhere. And like everything else in Lemming City, it's all thanks to me!"

Then he quickly added, as if a footnote, "And the New Ancients, of course."

"How many of these New Ancients venture outside?"

"There are so many heroes begging to get outside to complete our city that I can't even count the heroes!"

"Do you think that's safe out there in the frontier?"

"Of course, it's safe! We're building the finest security any lemming could ever imagine!"

Bigly's supporters, who were now beginning to move toward the back of the hall, couldn't resist breaking out into their usual chants. It continued for a while until Bigly waved them to quiet down because he had something important to share.

Before he had a chance to continue, Tez yelled out, "How many come back?"

It hit Bigly like a powerful blow. What did she know? Or was she just fishing around?

Bigly stood his ground. "All of them! Every single one!" Bigly was adept at denial.

"What about the ones Jobe and I saw being devoured by foxes yesterday?" Tez questioned.

"That's a lie!" he bellowed. "How dare you!"

"We saw it with our own eyes," Tez said.

"So why weren't you eaten as well?" Bigly said, feeling smug with his pithy reply.

"Because we outfoxed them!"

If Tez's first question was a body blow, the second came as a hard uppercut.

Bigly was panic-stricken. She knew too much. But Bigly, being Bigly, wouldn't take it sitting down, so he was going to come back fighting with his default defense: deny, deny, deny.

Before Tez had a chance to add anything else, Bigly's followers all started chanting, "Liar, Liar, Lair!" It escalated quickly into screams that reverberated throughout the hall and, in fact, could be heard throughout all of Lemming City. That's when some of Bigly's supporters started shoving the dissenters.

Bigly continued on maniacally, though it was barely audible above the din, "After all I have done for Lemmingtown! After building Lemming City! Why don't you all go and crawl back to your crappy little hole in the ground, or wherever it was that you came from and wither away, while we thrive here in Lemming City, the greatest city any lemming will ever know! And while you're at it, take all your loser friends with you."

Tez, Jobe, and her friends, along with many former Bigly fans, realized how this uncomfortable situation was quickly escalating out of control. It was worse than anything they could have ever imagined.

So they did what any intelligent lemming would do. Tez and Jobe scurried away one by one and pressed themselves tightly against the wall and headed toward the exit to Lemmingtown. All the others quickly followed by instinct, single file and scared out of their wits, but relieved that Tez had the courage to lead the way.

Bigly was still ranting, and the cheering was growing louder by the minute, but the going got easier as the crowd in the middle of the hall began thinning out to fill the space left behind by Tez and the others as they filed out.

As they passed by, more and more Lemmings joined them—perhaps Bigly and his most feverish supporters were now acting so crazily that many in the crowd had finally begun to recognize the sheer madness of it all.

Thirteen

(The Fall of Lemming City)

Lemming City was deeply flawed but even more than Tez and Jobe had first suspected. Its greatest weakness was not its lack of sentries nor any of winding narrow tunnels nor even the absence of any traps—it was Bigly Hall itself.

It might have been impressive enough, especially to Bigly and all his supporters, but little did any of them realize that this great cavern came with a hidden cost—the ceiling of Bigly Hall came dangerously close to the surface of the ground overhead.

Tez looked behind her and was amazed at the number of lemmings that were now following her. The noise from the hall had become deafening—Bigly's followers had now plunged themselves into some kind of bizarre ritualistic fervor. This was unlike any gathering before, and there was utter chaos throughout the hall—the kind that animals seem to display when some natural disaster is about to strike. It was like some reaction welling up to flee to higher ground or take refuge in a cave or burrow deep into the ground.

As the Grand Reveal raged on, the nighttime world above Bigly Hall was quiet and peaceful. Mr. Sid had been clever enough to have protected to his investment, and there were always at least a few foxes lingering around to fend off any competing predators, wolves excepted, but they rarely came around. In fact, much of the surrounding area had simply been passed over by predators long before because Lemmingtown, in contrast to Lemming City, had been so well constructed and so well hidden that the area had long been written off as devoid of any meaningful prey.

But it was on that night that two foxes who were supposed to be standing sentry had fallen asleep when a pair of weasels happened to pass by. The weasels had no interest in going anywhere near the area that was directly above Lemming City, especially because they could smell the foxes. But when they saw them sleeping, they thought they might be able to sneak past and make their way to better hunting grounds. They had heard there was plenty of food further north and decided to take a shortcut, even though it was not without a bit of risk. Weasels are clever that way, always shrewd in weighing risk with reward.

This time it paid off, and it had paid off in spades. Though no particular plan, other than risking slipping past a few sleeping foxes, they stumbled across the motherlode.

Moments after the weasels had started making their way across the meadow that was above Lemming City, they passed directly over Bigly Hall itself and could clearly make out the noise from all the crazy screaming at Bigly's Grand Reveal. They turned to each other and crooked their heads in a puzzled way. This was too good to be true. Their next meal was actually calling out to them.

The weasels glanced back to check that the foxes were still sleeping and started digging away at the ground—what else was a hungry weasel to do?

That's when it happened.

Inside the cavern, a few pieces of earth from the top of Bigly Hall fell to the floor somewhere near the middle of the room. The first weasel felt a crack open in the ground above. The ceiling inside the cavern began to crack, and the ground above it began to give way, and the sweet smell of sweaty lemming suddenly flooded the air outside.

"Run!" Tez screamed, and they all took flight, running as fast as they could, toward the safety of Lemmingtown.

Even though the growing crowd of dissidents behind her were panic-stricken, they were orderly as they poured down the tunnel single file without any of the pushing and shoving that had become commonplace at Bigly's gatherings.

The weasels up above began digging furiously. The crack widened until some of the ground beneath them collapsed. One of the weasels stuck his snout in the hole and started biting at anything he could sink its teeth into.

One of the foxes heard the ruckus in her sleep and managed to shake herself awake. She nipped the other one in the behind to rouse him and yelled, "If Mr. Sid ever hears out about this, we're done for!" They looked at each other and charged at the weasels. The first one sank her teeth into one of the weasels, and it let out a shriek.

"Hey!" the second fox yelled. "These are ours."

The second weasel bit into the second fox, never having been one to walk away from a fight. They went at it like cats and dogs, but the weasels didn't give up. The first one managed to cram himself underground and started to devour everything in sight.

That was when the next detail of foxes arrived on the scene, and the timing couldn't have been better—a moment earlier and the sentries would have been caught sleeping on the job. Instead, they were discovered valiantly fighting off the attack, and it would be something they would claim false credit for the rest of their lives and probably looked upon as heroes forever. That is simply because every part of every society has always had, and always will have, a little Bigly in it.

Just as Tez reached the outer perimeter of Lemmingtown, she stepped to one side and ushered the rest through the entrance with Jobe now leading the way. They all smiled and nodded to her as they sped out of Lemming City and back to the safety of Lemmingtown—there would be plenty of time to thank her later.

Tez turned back again and peered down the vast corridor that led to Bigly Hall.

It was at that moment when she witnessed the beginning of what would be the end of Lemming City—the crumbling ceiling completely collapsed.

There was nothing more she could do other than save the rest. So she turned back toward Lemmingtown and followed them home.

As Lemming City continued to crumble, a few of the lemmings scrambled to get outside through the gap in the ceiling, and many, many more began following them out.

Bigly stood over his creation—proudly proclaiming that he, and he alone, could save Lemming City. He ordered his followers to remain behind to defend his city, like some kind of banana republic dictator. But it was already too late, and while Bigly's charms had already worn thin even among many of his most ardent disciples, there were still many who stood their ground, refusing to give up on the futile struggle. It was as if they were pretending to be like devoted captains on a sinking ship. As his phony world continued to collapse all around him, all Bigly could think about was being loved by these idiots who would do anything for him.

Dweezil grabbed Bigly and said, "Sire, it's best if we leave now." He pulled Bigly off in the other direction—he knew an entrance to the outside world, far away from the mayhem. Bigly looked back, and the only thought that entered his mind was *What suckers.* The sight of all the carnage didn't disturb him in the slightest. In fact, he felt better for watching it because he was truly a malignant creature who only cared for himself.

Lemmings continued streaming out of the gaping hole the weasels had unearthed, and all the other foxes joined into what had become a feeding frenzy. There was no rationality behind any of it. They all wanted more, even though they already had more than enough.

The predators craved their prey as much as Bigly's supporters craved the drug he never failed to deliver.

Angel, the snowy owl, happened to be soaring high above and was startled at the sight of so many lemmings on the run but, apparently, to no place in particular. At first, she thought it might be dangerous, but after circling a few more times, she shrugged off her apprehension. This was the kind of all-you-can-eat buffet that would be crazy to ever pass up.

Angel was a lone predator who represented nature in its purest form. There was nothing phony about her—no societal niceties nor praising of false prophets. She had simply spotted a meal to be had and intended on taking it.

She swooped down with all the grace that Mother Nature had bestowed upon her. She levelled out and glided effortlessly behind one of the long lines not more than inches above the queue of fleeing lemmings. She spotted a couple of fat and juicy ones not far ahead and tucked her wings back for what would seem like nothing more than a blink of eye. It was elegant and graceful. It was natural. She latched on to a particularly plump one and soared up with her prey dangling limply, skewered through one of her talons, and she headed back to her nest.

Angel had built it high above the rocky cliffs where her three young snowy owls were waiting hungrily. She dropped her prey at their feet—it was a gift from their mother, and she intended it to be their last unearned meal.

She knew they still might be a little young to take flight, let alone turn into predators, but she also knew this opportunity to teach them was too great to pass up.

She allowed each of them a few pecks at the flesh and took some for herself. Then she gestured to the sky. The first two got the idea, and they jumped from the nest and took flight after a few unnerving midair tumbles, but she had to literally kick the third one out. They were all awkward at first, especially the third one, but in minutes, they were gliding effortlessly high above. It was truly nature at its best—owls merely doing what they were born to do. It was a refreshing contrast to everything Lemming City represented, which was unnatural and had been all on account of the selfish needs of one individual, facilitated by the stupidity of the mob he had infected. That individual was Bigly, the most unnatural of lemmings. He was the polar opposite of nature, and despite all his bravado, he was, without question, the worst of lemmings.

Angel climbed higher, with her little ones struggling to keep up, but this was how they would learn and grow their magnificent young bodies. High above the nest, Angel circled for a while, and they followed. She continued circling because she knew they deserved a well-earned rest, just soaring, circling around, up in the sky. Even from that great height and in the dark of night, it was impossible to miss the parades of lemmings streaming out of Lemming City in all directions.

She signaled them to follow her and learn how to hunt. They began their descent, with her young ones following alongside, well, more or less alongside, as the smallest had trouble controlling his speed at first. But it didn't take long for him to get the hang of it as well.

Angel led them lower and approached their prey from behind. The night sky was dark, so she knew there was no chance of revealing themselves with a shadow cast from moonlight.

She struck a nice fat one in the back of the neck, and the shock of witnessing it from behind caused the lemmings to scatter chaotically. Right behind her, the largest of the three owlets took a shot at imitating his mother. He copied her exactly and scooped up a small lemming and pulled up, struggling a little from the added weight his young wings now had to support. But he managed to climb, and Angel gestured for him to make his way back to the nest.

Angel was remarkably strong, and despite the weight of her fat prey, she circled back to see how the other two were making out—the middle one, her only daughter, was doing fine, but the smallest one was struggling near the surface.

Angel called out to her daughter, and she responded with conviction. She dropped her own catch and swooped back to help her little brother. The two of them seized a nice-sized one between them. They climbed slowly at first but eventually gained altitude and made their way back to the nest with Angel following close behind.

The hunt had been successful, and Angel was proud of how quickly her young had gained the skills that would soon make them self-sufficient. They had begun to transform themselves into proper predators. What was even more remarkable was how even predators could be capable of cooperating and sharing their spoils. There was a distinct lack of any Bigly-ness in them.

Lemmings continued to stream out of the collapsed cavern in panic-stricken parades of rodents fleeing in every direction. They merely followed one another, without having any kind of plan. Little did many of them realize they were headed toward the cliffs where Jobe and Tez had spent countless hours gazing out over the ocean and where the Ancients had first stopped short of so many generations before.

With the scent of lemming filling the air and blown by a light night breeze, it didn't take long to catch the attention of every predator within miles. Unfortunately for some of the predators, the unmistakable scent of lemming didn't go unnoticed by a few large wolves off in the distance. They knew that the smell would attract even larger prey for them and would be the ticket to a much more satisfying meal—why settle for some scrawny lemming when that smell would also attract creatures dozens of times larger?

It didn't take long before the thin covering of the ground above Lemming City had been completely ripped to shreds and predators from all around were feasting on all the lemmings they continued to uncover. Bigly loyalists continued to remain behind and stand their ground, even though their leader had long since abandoned them.

Deep inside Lemmingtown, all the lemmings who had been wise enough to follow Tez pushed further into the town, well past all the traps and pitfalls.

Tez knew that Lemmingtown had now been compromised and that it wouldn't take long before it was ransacked as well.

They needed to act fast. She had caught up with the front of the line and then stopped and turned back.

"Wait!" she yelled. "We know a safe place! It's a gift to us from the Ancients! Follow us!"

Jobe turned to her, and he nodded and smiled—his hunch had been right all along, and Tez had assumed the mantle with ease.

The Ancients had been wise. All their careful planning and anticipation that their world wasn't permanent, and should never be taken for granted, had sadly come to pass.

The time had come for Lemmingtown to begin again—to return to its old values and to what had made it great in the first place. It would be a struggle at first, and there would be hardship, but it was an essential struggle and one that would ensure the future of the town and its remaining inhabitants.

Tez and Jobe led the way to Kit's old room where they had reemerged into Lemmingtown only that morning, and it all suddenly made sense to them.

Lemmingtown could have survived forever. But now that it had been compromised, it was already too late—Bigly had ruined everything.

The reason why the Ancients had left those caves unoccupied became abundantly clear. It was an escape hatch into a new sanctuary.

Fourteen

(Return to the Cliffs)

The refugees from Lemming City had embraced their new home from the very start and had nurtured it carefully from its simple beginnings.

Life wasn't easy at first—living in caves of eroded rock—but they knew them to be safe and completely impregnable. The floors and walls were cold at first, but it didn't take long before more and more survivors ventured out briefly into the woods. They had to squeeze themselves through the same cracks as Jobe and Tez had on their fateful return to Lemmingtown. They always returned with just enough food for everyone and plenty of twigs and bark to insulate their new home.

Memories of the collapse of Lemming City had seemed to evaporate almost overnight—the perception of time has a strange way of changing during times of upheaval and dire stress. Life in *Old Lemmingtown*, as they all now called it, quickly returned to one of tranquility and harmony. It was exactly as Lemmingtown had always been, or at least until Bigly had corrupted and degraded it. Of course, there were bound to be occasional minor squabbles, but that had been just as much a part of life in Lemmingtown as it would be in any normal society.

The refugees were just happy to be alive and having created new lives for themselves. They were truly the genuine New Ancients, although they would never dream of thinking of themselves that way, nor would they ever wish to be remembered like that. They had simply recreated their former home and were not trying to live out some marketing-slogan vision of a self-indulgent lunatic.

In short, the spirit and soul of Lemmingtown had survived—it had only moved next door.

Tez and Jobe worked diligently on trying to uncover the meanings of the strange inscriptions scratched into the walls every day. Tez was still learning, and Jobe, although slightly further along, was still learning as well. It was a never-ending challenge, and with each re-reading, they gleaned their own new insights.

The refugees continued to work tirelessly at rebuilding their old lives.

They decided to adopt a set of guidelines—the same ones that Lemmingtown had lived by for ages but without ever having been clearly spelled out. This was not some kind of authoritarian decree as Bigly would have had it. They simply wanted to reinforce the rules they had always lived by, and all agreed to formally carve out a set of principles that would define Old Lemmingtown and enable it to continue forever.

They decided to scratch them inside the rocky cavern across from the narrow crack in the rocks that would forever serve as their gateway to the outside world.

They began by smoothing out a small place on the wall that would be the first thing any lemming would see when they entered Old Lemmingtown, and on it, they inscribed,

Let no Lemming Enter,
Who is Ignorant of Our Ways.
We are Equals,
We are Selfless,
We are Stronger Together,
Than by Following Any False Prophet.

After their work had been completed, there was no ceremony nor were there any cheering crowds. There was no rush of endorphins simply because Old Lemmingtown was a reflection of who these lemmings truly were and always had been: simple, modest, and unpretentious.

Time had marched on, and early one morning Jobe passed by the tiny space where Tez now slept. She had already been awake for hours and followed him instinctively. It was comforting because it reminded her of all the times she had followed Jobe out to the cliff.

He led her to the foyer that had become the gateway to the outside world, and they stopped in front of the inscription. They stood silently side by side and gazed at it.

It was probably only for moments, but it felt like hours to Tez.

Jobe turned to her and smiled.

All the wisdom of the ancient texts suddenly flooded her consciousness, and she felt more tranquility and peacefulness than ever before.

She stepped closer to the wall and paused for a moment.

She looked up and reflected on it for one last time and then scratched out a little symbol from one of the ancient texts that captured all of what the citizens of Old Lemmingtown would eventually figure out for themselves.

Tez realized it might be difficult for them to grasp it at first, but she also knew that everyone in Old Lemmingtown would eventually understand what it meant. It represented all that had been lacking in Lemming City: peace, love, and harmony.

Jobe stepped forward and stood beside her. He gazed at this wonderful wall then turned and nodded to her, and she knew the time had come.

Jobe crammed his way into the crack at the far side of the entryway, and Tez followed close behind.

Just before she disappeared inside, she turned her head back to take one last look at the wall and saw two young Lemmings staring at her inscription.

They turned to her, and she smiled at them.

She forced herself into the crack and squeezed through the fissures until she finally caught up with Jobe.

The familiar blue glow that had been her guiding light was now completely surrounding Jobe, and she quickly realized it was all around her as well.

Jobe turned to her and said, "We're going to be fine now."

"I know," she said, "and I finally understand."

"That strange verse?"

"Yes," she said. "It came to me in a dream last night."

"You will be safe now," Jobe said.

"Yes, I know."

"But the time has come," Jobe said.

"I understand," she said.

They pushed themselves through the final crack and out into the outside world and began their journey back to the cliffs.

There were many predators out on the prowl that night, but Tez and Jobe were protected by the glow.

When they reached the entrance to the clifftop caves, the glow was beginning to wane, so they hurried inside. Tez rubbed herself against the pee-saturated moss and briefly ventured back outside to rub the scent over some of the rocks and trees in case any curious predators might have followed them.

Back inside, Tez and Jobe spoke again.

"I liked the glow better," Tez said.

Jobe laughed a little and said, "I know, but apparently, it only appears when absolutely necessary."

"I guess we'll just have to put up with the stink," Tez said.

"Yes, I guess you will," Jobe said, "but I'm sure you will figure it out."

That would be the last time they would speak.

On the way inside, past the pit and all the turns and traps, Jobe paused for a moment and gestured toward a small cavern that Tez hadn't noticed when they had first left.

She looked inside and realized what it was. It was the final resting place of the Legacies.

She turned back to Jobe and stared deeply into his eyes. They were serene and calm and loving. He smiled at her, and she smiled back, for they knew that the torch had finally been passed from one generation of Legacies to the next.

Jobe's final wish was that Tez would never have to be tested that way again. But he also knew that she could take on any challenge that might come her way.

Tez knew this too, and as they made their way through the passages and back toward their old rooms, a feeling of warmth flowed over them. They stopped at Tez's room first as Jobe's lay further ahead. He turned to her and nodded. It was as if to say goodbye but without spoiling the moment with unnecessary words. Her eyes had already been welling with tears, and she simply nodded back, with all the dignity and respect that she could summon.

Tez woke early the next morning, waiting in vain that Jobe might somehow miraculously pass by and lead her out to the cliffs.

But she knew this was not to be.

She went down to check his room anyway, and when she saw he was gone, she knew where he was and that this room would be hers from now on.

She thought about her old room and wondered about who its next occupant might be and what might bring them there.

She wondered about Bigly and if he had been eaten or had somehow managed to slip away into the night.

But she didn't dwell on any of it for long. Instead, she simply turned away and headed toward the cliffs.

This time she was on her own, just as Jobe must have done every day for so very long. She scurried at first and then started to run. She ran past her old room. She ran faster and faster toward the cliffs where she had learned so much from Jobe. After that one last turn to the right, she burst out of the darkness and into the light.

It was just as the sun was about to rise.

January 6, 2022

CPSIA information can be obtained
at www.ICGtesting.com
Printed in the USA
LVHW032325300622
722528LV00003B/359